# Only Sound Remains

# Only Sound Remains

## Hossein Asgari

PUNCHER & WATTMANN

First published in 2023
Published by Puncher and Wattmann
PO Box 279
Waratah NSW 2298

https://www.puncherandwattmann.com
web@puncherandwattmann.com

ISBN   9781922571731

Cover design by Moe Hashemian
Typesetting by Morgan Arnett
Printed by Lightning Source International

 A catalogue record for this work is available from the National Library of Australia

*They will utter with their tongues something that is not in their hearts.*
  *—Al-Fath [48:11]*


*The little quantum of truth that is any use to you, you receive gratis and for nothing; and if it is mixed with lies and errors, this too is for your health's sake; undiluted, it would sear your entrails. Don't try to purge your soul of lies, so much else you didn't think of will follow in their wake; you'll only lose yourself, and all that's dear to you. "Thou shalt not ask!"*
  *—Hjalmar Söderberg,* Doctor Glas

For Maman and Baba,
who read to me when I couldn't

# Chapter One

The last lines of the story came to me with the last sip of my coffee.

*…He closes his eyes.*
*The concrete city hums—keeping rhythm with the thuds of his mechanical heart.*

I'd collected my laptop to rush to my next tutorial when my phone rang. It was my mother, excited to let me know that my father had decided to pay me a visit. "I can't believe it," she said. "I thought I'd die before seeing him travel."

"Yeah, it's not like him at all." I threw my backpack on my shoulder.

"You there?"

"Yes."

"Aren't you happy?"

"Of course I am."

The news of my father's travel unsettled me. It triggered something inside me and I started thinking about Payam again, his disappearance and his death. Guilt. Regret. Remorse. I found myself arguing with him, trying to justify my decision or convince him to change his. I found myself talking to his mother to console her. I found myself—lost.

I wanted the pointless emotional struggle to stop, but I wasn't in charge anymore. The old me, the real me, pushed down and hidden under a facade of normality, started taking over again. Every day my reflection became more like the man who had entered this country five years ago in search of freedom, peace, and a chance for a fresh start, only to realise nothing was harder than escaping one's destiny.

I wanted Payam to leave me alone. "Not today, buddy! Not today," I said, but he seemed not to care. His presence disrupted the routine that had helped me to forge a sense of balance. I missed a dance class here, a running session there, and ended up in bars at the time I'd allocated to writing for the last three years. I wanted my life back, the one I'd built to leave the old one behind, so I started taking EFFEXOR again, the pills that had remained in the fridge from two years ago. In a few weeks, I was ready to greet my father with a smile.

In the airport, kids were chasing one another; beautiful women lingered in colourful dresses; two old men were sipping their coffees; Payam was lurking in the shadows; I thought about the dream I'd had last night. I was in a concrete pit, deep enough so I couldn't touch the rim even when I jumped. Every second a droplet of water fell in from an invisible tap. Eventually I was going to drown. How had I ended up in the pit? I'd fallen in while running. From what? I didn't know. Hands on the wall, head drooping between shoulders, I closed my eyes and breathed slowly to hold back the panic, but it washed over me like a wave and I woke up with a gasp.

"Saeed!"

One thousand, seven hundred days. My father had grown older than I expected. Thin and humpy, uniformly white unkempt hair, bony face. Only his eyes were the same: vivid and bright. No matter how old we grow, something remains untouched, something that pours out of our eyes. Is that why some believe in soul? I got to my feet and hugged him. We stayed like that for a moment or two. In silence.

"How are you?" I asked.

"I'm alright. Did you have to wait for long?"

"Not really. How was your flight?"

"I took two sleeping pills, so I didn't notice much."

"How's Mum doing?" I took his luggage out of his hand.

The light in his eyes disappeared. They filled with something incomprehensible, something unpleasant. Anger? Disappointment? I couldn't pin it down.

"She's okay," he murmured.

"No way she could've come?" I asked knowing the answer.

"Doctor said it would be suicide. It's pretty hot here," he exhaled.

"It's one of those summer nights." The warm air breathed into my face. "How's Roozbeh?"

"You know your brother. He's alright, as long as nothing interrupts his routine."

"How's Hamid doing?"

"He's good. Has he told you that he won a prize for one of his translations?"

"Yeah. He sent me a copy of the book," I said. It's good that he has his favourite son on his side. "Welcome to Adelaide." I forced a smile. He nodded and kept walking. "We have to take a cab on the other side."

"Let's catch a bus if it's cheaper."

"It's okay, I earn more than enough," I lied. What I paid for my studio apartment ate up most of my income.

On the way home, my father looked out of the cab window. I leaned my head back and distorted lights rushed into the window frame as I struggled to keep my eyes open.

"Saeed—" I turned my head to see the same unpleasant look, the one I saw when I asked about my mother "—is it worth it?"

I knew what he meant, but I still asked, "What do you mean?"

He turned his head and let his gaze take asylum in the colours of the night.

*

I took out two chairs to the small balcony and we sat.

"You look tired," he said.

"Had a long day." I pressed my palms to my eyes.

"Still tutoring maths?"

"Yeah."

"You should look for a permanent job. Having a work routine keeps one healthy and out of trouble."

"I *am* looking," I lied. The idea of a nine-to-five job made me anxious.

"Even with a full-time job you can still write."

"I know."

"Are you working on anything new?"

He never showed much interest in my writing. "A short story."

"About?"

"A man who wakes up in a hospital to realise that his heart has been replaced by a mechanical one."

"Why?"

"It's not complete yet."

"You have to let him go."

"It's not about him, Baba! Can we talk about something else?"

We chatted about family and friends, looking at the city's flickering lights. Newborn babies, the recently deceased, newlyweds, and at one point, my cousin's new car. It took less than an hour. I wasn't surprised that we had little to talk about. I couldn't expect too much connection on a personal level with someone who only felt at ease in his room, reading, or in the yard, gardening, even if he was my father.

Still, I was aware that as long as I didn't answer my father's question— the one I had avoided in the cab—we would go from one awkward silence to another.

"I had to write it," I said eventually. Payam was my best friend and he'd disappeared into the thin air as if he'd never existed. And I didn't do anything. I didn't look for him because I was scared. Like a coward! I started writing about it because I had no choice. Writing about his death was the only way to have closure and to be able to go on.

"I have nothing against you writing that novel. But you didn't have to publish it. It's too damn political! You knew that if you published it you might not be able to come back and you still did it. You may never see your country, your family, friends and most important of all, your mother again. *Was it worth it?*"

I have left everything and everyone I knew and cared for behind, so I could live, love and write freely, I could live with dignity. Have I gotten what I was after? Was it worth it? Why did I publish the book? Was it that I didn't want to admit that 20,000 kilometres away, I was still afraid of them? Did I wish for people to know his story? Or did I feel guilty and want to punish myself? Was I simply being driven by my own vanity? Regardless, I have made a decision and now I have to live with its consequences. But was it worth it?

I took a sip of my tea and kept quiet.

"It's time I slept," he said.

*

I struggled to sleep. I felt Payam's presence, the night I talked to him for the last time, the clock showing 9:00pm sharp. He'd called to ask me to attend the protest organised for the next day, the one expected to be the biggest since the rigged—so many believed—presidential election. I told him I wasn't going, and in my opinion neither should he. If we'd learnt one thing from our history, which repeated itself again and again, it was that nothing would come out of all these struggles unless… He hadn't called for my *valuable* conservative inputs, he said, but my support which he now knew he couldn't count on. The conversation was short and left me embittered. Now my chest tightens every time a clock shows 9 o'clock, every time the answer to an equation turns out to be nine, or nineteen, or ninety, every time the number nine appears on a bill… Nine had been one of my favourite numbers.

My father woke me in the middle of the night. He wanted to pray and asked about *qiblah*. He couldn't find his *qiblah* locator and kept repeating that he was sure he'd put it in his damn luggage. Hazy with sleep, I had no idea which direction Mecca was. I pointed towards the balcony, the studio's sliding glass window. At least it had a nice view.

*

The next morning my father wanted to stay in and take rest for the day. He lay in bed reading *A Modern History of Iran,* which he'd borrowed from my collection, with a cup of tea on the bedside table. I sat behind my desk preparing myself for the afternoon's sessions. But having remembered that I'd forgotten to buy cooking oil, I left the apartment for the convenience store just a few blocks away.

When I came back and put the oil in the cabinet my father was still in bed, but I couldn't rid myself of the afterimage of a scene I'd glimpsed as I entered the studio: my father sliding something under the blanket before picking up the book he'd been reading previously.

I started cooking when he was in the shower. "Baba jan, do you mind if I add some mushrooms to the omelet?" He didn't hear me over the sound of water. I left the mushrooms in the sink to arrange his bed. I was surprised at what I found under the blanket. I put it back and rearranged everything as it was.


There should be nothing surprising about a retired teacher of Persian literature carrying a *diwan* of poetry. However, the one I'd just found under his blanket belonged to one of the most controversial poets in contemporary Persian literature. A woman. When I'd heard her name for the first time during my teenage years, my father's library—home to almost all the most significant Persian poetry collections, both classic and contemporary—was the first place I looked for her poetry. I couldn't find them in his library. I vaguely remembered asking my father if he had any of her books, as they were out of print and banned at the time. He must have said no, since I bought a pirated copy on the black market. Now, here was one of the oldest ever published copies of her collected poetry under his blanket.

Quite intriguing that my father, who had always expressed affection in the most controlled manner—if at all—had come all this way and brought only one book, one by Forough Farrokhzad: the poet of worldly love.

6

I glanced at the copy of the English translation of Forugh's selected works in my bookshelf. It sat next to my own novel, *The Imaginary Narrative of a Real Murder*. One thousand copies published, even less sold. I picked it up and skimmed through. "To Payam and all the disobedient sons," read the first page. The next page narrated the gist of a Persian myth in which the legendary Rostam unwittingly kills his own long-lost son on a battlefield. At the bottom of the page, I'd jotted one of Forugh's verses down, which during my depression after Payam's disappearance I'd recited constantly.

*Life perhaps is a rope*
*with which a man*
*hangs himself from a branch.*

\*

The second day, I took my father to the beach. Since his arrival, I'd been waiting for bad news and the ocean, nonchalant and sublime, always eased my sense of foreboding. My father hated travelling and had never left Iran except for the Mecca pilgrimage. In my first year in Australia I'd tried for weeks to persuade him to join my mother, who was coming to visit me—since she would have a hard time travelling alone—but his answer was always no. Now here he was, four years later, when my mother was too sick to travel and he seemed weak and tired all the time. Something was terribly wrong; why else would he bother travelling all this way?

"Wait for a second," I said as we got off the tram. I put sunscreen on his face. "Rub it all over. The sun here's a killer."

"You need to be much younger than me to have enough time to be killed by the sun."

I took off my shoes and socks. He kept his on. We walked on the beach listening to the ocean. In a few minutes, small beads of sweat were rolling down his forehead to be blocked by his thick eyebrows.

"Do you want a cold drink?" He nodded. We walked away from the beach to the pavement and stayed under the shade of a palm tree. "Wait here for me." I ran towards a convenience store. When I got back he was standing at the same spot, in the same posture. I passed him a ginger beer. He took a sip of his drink. "I just talked to Ellie and she said hi."

"Say hi to her for me," he said. Waiting for more, I didn't respond. Since yesterday, I'd been waiting for him to ask about her, to acknowledge her presence in my life. He knew how important she was to me. It was only after meeting her that my life had slowly turned from being a day-to-day struggle, carried on only with the help of EFFEXOR, my little pink friends. "How's she doing?" he asked, as if feeling compelled.

"She's well, but nowadays she has to travel a lot for work. Her firm wanted her to stay a bit longer in Brisbane, but she negotiated her return so she could meet you before you left."

"Good, good," he said.

We finished our drinks and walked back to the beach. I stood near the sea and let the water wash the heat off my feet. He stayed back, not to get his shoes wet.

"When was the last time you were by the sea?"

"Long time ago."

"It's beautiful, isn't it?"

"Yes," he said absentmindedly.

"Do you want to swim?" He stared at the sea and didn't respond. "Are you hungry?" It was early to eat, but there wasn't much to say or to do.

"I could eat."

"What do you feel like having?"

"Let's have fish. That's the only halal food one can get here, I guess," he said.

"Mum always cooked fish for the New Year."

"No one can cook a better fish than she does."

"There are some fish-and-chip shops near the tram station."

"Good. Let's have fish for lunch. I don't think we can find any other halal food here."

"Sure. Fish for lunch," I said, a bit surprised. A ghost of something like

8

embarrassment shimmered in his eyes.

He waited at a table outside the shop. When I came out, he was staring at an oil stain on the table.

"There you go, fish and chips with tartare sauce."

He snapped back to the present. "Thanks." He took a bite.

"Is it good?"

"Very fresh. Eat!"

"You eat first."

"Aren't you hungry?"

"You go ahead. I'll eat some chips."

"Chips?"

"I'm not eating meat."

He looked at me in perplexity. "If you don't like fish go and get whatever you like."

"I like fish. I just don't eat meat."

"Why? Are you sick or something?"

"No. I just think it's wrong." He stared at me as if he couldn't believe what he had heard. "Enjoy your food. I'll eat later."

"What's wrong with eating meat?"

"For me, it's this sense of entitlement, the entitlement to flesh. It's a bit like rape… I'm sorry, forget it! Let's talk about it later. Eat it before it gets cold."

"What is it? One of these new-age trends?"

I kept quiet. He took a few bites before he stopped. I looked at him rubbing his agitated fingers on a tissue. I wanted to say, "I thought you were hungry, don't you want to finish it?" But I kept quiet. I couldn't think of anything, to do or to say, to make him feel better.

\*

The third day, I woke up to see him leaning back in his bed reading Forugh's *diwan*.

"Do you have a class today?"

"No," I answered, trying to mask my surprise.

"I need to tell you something, but let's eat breakfast first."

Here it comes, I thought. And right when I had started thinking that perhaps he had only come to visit me after all. At breakfast, he spoke only once, when he followed my gaze to Forugh's *diwan* lying on the bed, left open in the middle.

"I'll explain that too."

I collected the dishes and put them in the sink.

"Make yourself comfortable. It might take a while," he said.

"What's this about, Baba? You're making me worried."

"Nothing to worry about."

I took out my study chair and sat on it, feeling uncomfortable, like somebody who was getting ready to be cross-examined. He sat on the bed and picked up the *diwan*.

> *My whole being is a dark verse which*
> *—while chanting you—*
> *will take you to the dawn*
> *of eternal growth and blossoming.*
> *In this verse, I sighed you, ah!*
> *In this verse, I grafted you*
> *to the tree and the water and the fire.*

"It's beautiful," he said after a pause. "Have you ever wondered who the mentioned *you* is?"

"*Another birth* is dedicated to I. G., and people say it's Ibrahim Golestan."

"It's interesting that it's the same initials as for my name—Ismael Golzar. I know it's not me, but I wish it was," he smiled. A fleeting bitter smile.

"What do you mean?"

"Her father's house was only a few blocks down the road from ours, at the dead end of our alley. I was four years younger than Forugh, and…"

He squinted, as though he was trying to see something clearer.

"And?"

She and God entered my life almost at the same time.

The summer that she returned to our neighbourhood after living in Ahvaz for a few years, and I saw her again this time in a new light, I also joined my father to pray at the mosque for the first time. Soon, I grew fond of congregational prayers. I felt as if I was part of something larger than life and death, larger than the universe. Something was sweeping through the centuries before drowning my body and soul, washing away all my petty needs and desires. I wished for that serene ecstasy to last forever, but life and its realities kicked in as soon as I stepped outside.

I admired the imam of the mosque, Ayatollah Entezari. He was tall, well-built, with a broad wrinkle-free forehead, an everlasting smile, and a solid reputation for benevolence and generosity. It was through his religious sermons that I truly learnt about sin: that it wasn't something abstract. Our actions, wills, even our most private thoughts and desires could interact with the material world, have consequences, and bring God's blessing or torment. The first time I shook his hand and asked a religious question, I never thought it was the beginning of a strange friendship between a teenager and a middle-aged man which would last for many years.

And then there was her. I only read her poem by accident—the one responsible for all the furore. I saw the title of the magazine, *The Intellectual*, when Zari snatched it out of Zohre's hands. "Let me see her picture!"

"What are you looking at, Ismael? Aren't you supposed to be at the shop?" Zohre said when she noticed me. She was only 19 and five years younger than Zari, but was already married and five months pregnant.

"I'm not going to work today," I mumbled. "I've twisted my ankle."

My sisters would never buy a magazine named *The Intellectual*. Later that day, I sneaked into Zari's room and found the magazine hidden under her mattress. The piece, entitled "The bold poet", had a biography, a poem, and a picture. Her eyes couldn't conceal the insecurity beneath, and her smile, as if subdued right before turning full and complete, revealed a thin streak of white teeth. I checked the picture and examined every detail, from the strand of hair on the forehead to the shapely lips, before moving to the text. It introduced Forugh as one of the youngest poets of Iran. She'd quit high school when she fell in love and got married. Now she lived with her husband and her two-year old baby boy in Ahvaz. She wished for women's social progress and the freedom to express themselves without fear of being ostracised. The article concluded with a poem: "Sin". I read it in one breath.

*I sinned, a gratifying sin,*
*in an embrace, warm and ardent,*
*I sinned embraced by arms,*
*hot and vindictive and iron.*
*In that dark and silent seclusion,*
*I looked into his mysterious eyes*
*my heart trembled impatiently in my chest*
*by the desires in his yearning eyes.*
*In that dark and silent seclusion,*
*I sat anxiously at his side,*
*his lips poured desire on my lips,*
*I escaped the sorrow of the crazed heart.*
*I read into his ear the tale of love*
*I want you, O, my dearest,*
*I want you, O, life-giving embrace,*
*O, you, my frenzied lover…*

My heart pounded, my face burned with shame, I read it word by word over and again. Zohre must've borrowed it from a friend, since it was an older issue, published a while back. I had a feeling that this document of infamy had passed through many hands. Its journey wasn't about to end yet.

I copied the poem down on a piece of paper and hid it under my mattress. Every day I took it out of its hiding spot and read it again. I was the man in the poem. Into my ear, she whispered her tale of love; in my embrace, she sought life. She: black eyes, a thread of hair almost touching her lips—slightly open, withered, waiting for a kiss to bring them back to life. She was my love. She was a disgrace. She was my love. She was a harlot. She was my love. She was … my sin.

*

My father stopped his narrative, and walked to the cabinet to fix himself a cup of tea. "Where do you keep your teabags?"

"Right there, in the first drawer."

"When we speak about humans, we try to explain the unexplainable—" he dipped a teabag in his cup and stayed still for a few seconds "—we go round and round as we talk and speculate with a serious frown on our face that makes us look ridiculous, when the so-called truth with its shady suspicious existence or with all its non-existence sits at the centre with a smile on her face that reads: I know things that you don't!"

He sat back and stared at the white cup in his hand. A minute or so passed. He inhaled the jasmine-scented steam. "The smell of spring. It always brings to life the first vivid image I have of her."

*

Her white floral chador was twirling in the wind, revealing some of her skin, as Forugh passed by us kids playing on the street. Somebody shouted my name; my gaze dropped down her dancing chador, and I kicked the ball clumsily. It hit her ankle and bounced back. She turned her head and smiled at me.

I knew she was in love. I had heard my sisters gossiping about Forugh and Parviz, who was 27 and 11 years older than her. Parviz had asked for her hand, but neither of the families were in favour of the marriage. Forugh was persistent though. That was all I'd heard about that love story and as a 12 year-old boy I couldn't care less.

She walked by Davud and he turned towards us, crossed his eyes, puckered his lips, kissed the air, curled up his fingers and jerked them back and forth in front of his penis. Hasan—Forugh's playmate before she was

13

considered too old to play with boys—shook his head in reproach and walked away. Davud shouted, "Hey faggot! If you walk away, you won't come back! Never!" I despised Davud. But I wanted to be part of the gang and joined in laughing with everybody else.

After weeks of crying and days of hunger strikes, she finally got married. It was a simple ceremony with only close relatives and a few neighbours. Soon after the wedding, she moved to Ahvaz with her husband.

*

I forgot that she existed until one summer night at dinner, when I was fifteen, I heard Forugh had returned from Ahvaz to stay at her father's house. The next-door neighbours had heard Forugh screaming and crying and her father shouting furiously—a divorce seemed certain.

"This Farrokhzad family never fails to make a scene," my mother said, and others joined in telling stories of their disgrace.

There was something seriously wrong with Forugh from the very beginning. She'd attempted suicide during her teenage years—twice! She was lucky a physician lived nearby, otherwise she wouldn't have made it.

What about the time they'd awakened the whole neighbourhood? Forugh's mother, Turan, ambushed her husband's second wife, beat her, and dragged her on the ground by her hair. When people rushed into the street after hearing all the yelling and screaming and managed to separate them, Turan held a clump of hair in her hand.

The gossip went on after dinner and over tea.

Didn't Forugh choose her husband? Why divorce, then? She had a good-looking spouse, financial security, a baby boy. What else did she want from her life? She seemed incapable of living a peaceful, quiet life. And the poem! Who would publish such brazen nonsense as poetry? When Forugh published that so-called poem, Parviz didn't go to work out of shame for two weeks. He should've divorced her straight away after kicking her out of the house. However, he didn't do anything and Forugh came back to Tehran in a couple of months and had a contract for her first book as if nothing

14

had happened. The neighbours had seen her right before she went back to Ahvaz with a few boxes in her hand. Gifts for her husband and son, Kami, to celebrate her book contract with them.

Turan swore to God that she'd asked Parviz not to give his wife too much freedom. He ignored her advice; now look at all the scandals: the poem, the shameless man, and now the divorce…

Even your grandfather who didn't usually tolerate gossip listened in silence. What poem were they talking about? Which shameless man? What had he done? I didn't ask. I knew that no one would deign to answer a teenager's question on such sensitive matters.

*

During the summer holidays, I worked at my father's grocery shop. That afternoon I was coming down with a flu and he sent me home to rest. I turned a corner and there she was. A white chador, imprinted with tiny grey leaves, sitting loosely on her head and showing her marble neck. Her slender fingers rested between her breasts to hold her hijab as it danced with the wind and played hide and seek with her skin.

Her steps weren't as brisk as the last time I'd seen her and something about her gaze had changed. Grown more melancholic? Matured? I couldn't tell. Her body wasn't one of a teenager either, and she looked more like a woman. When she passed me by, I turned without thinking and followed her, listening to the pounding of my heart. My eyes, burning with fever, followed the gentle movements of her buttocks masked by the soft fabric of her chador. She suddenly stopped, turned, and I hid behind a tree until I was sure she was gone.

I ran back home and for the first time in my life did what Davud had once pantomimed. Surprised with pleasure and overwhelmed with guilt, my body burned with fever. I was in hell for a week.

After that I didn't miss any chance to sneak out of my father's shop or to hang around the streets hoping to see her again. I had no other encounter with her during that summer, but she'd turned into the reason for my restlessness, the temptation, and the unbearable guilt. I hated her. Thinking of those dark black eyes and subtle smile, my heart grew soft. I loved her.

*

I asked my friends from the street about the scandalous poem, trying to bring it up as casually as possible. They knew nothing.

"I climbed the tree in front of her parents' house and I could see right through her bedroom," Davud said. "She knew I was there but didn't care. She started changing into her gown…"

You are lying, you pathetic goat-fucker! I thought. Still, I couldn't refrain from listening to his dirty story.

I snuck out of the house when the city was asleep and stood at the tree in Davud's story night after night. What if I climbed it and somebody saw me? I couldn't think of any excuse for what I was about to do. Always I returned home angry with myself, Davud, Forugh and the whole world. Davud was a liar and not a good one, but I still had to know, had to be sure.

Finally one night I took a deep breath, grabbed the lowest branch, pulled myself up, and climbed until I had a clear view of the windows into two large rooms at the other side of the yard. One almost dark room with a sizeable bookshelf: the father's. A silhouette of a man, sitting on a rocking chair, motionless, reading. Another one, the mother's, lit with a dim light and full of dolls. A middle-aged woman was sitting on the bed, combing the golden hair of a big doll in a white bridal gown. There was something spooky, eerie, about the room, the shadows, the slow motion of the woman's hand and her half-smile. A bizarre feeling started swirling in my stomach: *crazy doll lady!* I was trying to remember where and when I'd heard that phrase when she raised her head. Without thinking, I slid on my butt and hung from the branch for a second before I let go.

Jumping from the tree, I sprained my foot, but even the pulsing pain in my ankle couldn't stop me from thinking about her. I'd heard that if you focused all your mental energy on a wish it would come true. I wished I could see her again soon. I didn't get the wish, but the following day while I hobbled around the house, my sisters were fussing over "Sin".

*

At times, I managed to ignore the poem written on a piece of recycled brown paper hidden under my mattress, but not for long. The urge to take it out and read it would return. There was something about the poem, about the description of two bodies coming together for no higher purpose but their desire, that every cell in my body agreed with.

"Sin" fed into my obsession, kept her vivid and alive in my mind, and set my imagination free. In my fantasies I wasn't a hopeless teenager, but assured and confident. We made love over and again until I knew every curve, every taste, every touch. I lived and even grew old with her. The only other companion in that blessed imaginary life of mine was guilt.

I tried to compensate for my sinful fantasies with good deeds. I would fast for a few days in a row, wake up in the middle of the night to pray and throw money into charity boxes. I would wander around the streets of Tehran helping people: carrying an old lady's groceries; offering help in a mosque I'd never been to; giving a hand to disabled people on the street. These acts of benevolence temporarily silenced the accusing voice in my head—ancient, grave, and imposing—which kept reminding me that *my body* was wrong, *he* was right.

# Chapter Two

"Let's have a break," my father said.

We left for a nearby park.

Hard to imagine my father as a young man capable of such desire. Hard to believe that under that furrowed forehead and inscrutable face still lived the memory of a love that hadn't left him alone all these years. What is it that you were willing to travel all this way to share? Why would a man like you, always so dignified, so proper, tell his son about lusting after an older woman (and not any woman but Forugh) as a teenager? I wanted to say something, to ask questions. However, having seen my father talking openly about his past and his feelings, I felt strained, the way I did around strangers. My sense of foreboding was back—stronger than ever.

His description of Forugh's hijab was peculiar too. Pictures I had seen of her showed that she wasn't covering her head. Maybe that day she was wearing a chador for some unknown reason. Not to attract attention as a divorcee? To go to one of the holy shrines around Tehran? Or maybe, after decades, the picture had changed in my father's mind?

"There are plenty of green spots all over the city," my father said as we entered the park. "It gives people, ordinary people, so much space. You can't grow without space."

We walked around the park without uttering another word. We were quiet not because I felt uneasy and didn't know what to say, but because he knew silence was his friend while every word, like a small treacherous Judas, unveiled him. He wished to maintain the silence for now and to convey his wish he didn't need to use his words—as if, hiding behind this silence his entire life, he'd mastered its language. We sat on a bench near a lake.

He took out the packet of bread we'd bought and started feeding the ducks. At one point, I saw him staring at a spot on the lake and throwing the pieces of bread absentmindedly. I pretended that I hadn't noticed anything, bending forward towards the lake, putting my fists under my chin, watching the chaos in the lake with the ducks quacking and fighting. Without turning my head, I sneaked a peek at him. He jolted out of his reverie and looked at the almost empty packet of bread. A blush crawled up his neck and disappeared under his beard before he put the bread back in the shopping bag and broke the silence.

*

I'd learnt from Ayatollah Entezari that the accumulation of people's sins could bring God's wrath upon them. When I said that to my history teacher at school—who was speaking about the demise of the Sasanian Empire—he said, as if talking to himself, "Then with all the corruption, injustice and tyranny, this city must be flattened on a daily basis."

The earthquake of our sins eventually came when I was in one of the bookshops that I frequented, waiting for Forugh's first book to be finally out. I was leafing through a book, and trying to avoid eye contact with the salesman who was curious about the teenager who came to his shop every day, browsed books in silence, and left without buying anything or uttering a word.

I was standing next to the shop display window when it began to vibrate. The ground under my feet joined in harmony and I thought, Here it comes! I could hear crying, screaming, and shattering, as if a sudden hell had broken out of the unwavering peace of a minute ago. I stood frozen with fear. The salesman shouted "Come here!" and beckoned me to join him behind the desk. The book in my hand hit the ground. I looked over my shoulder and saw the gun of a tank slowly appearing in the window frame. A brick shattered the window and a rain of luminous glass flew towards me. Bending over, I ran for the desk and hunched next to the salesman. In a minute or two when we peeked over the desk, the newspaper stall at the other side of the street was on fire.

"Don't move!" the salesman said. He raised his hand and pulled a piece of glass out of my face. A sting, and the warm trace of blood ran down my cheek. He took a handkerchief, folded neatly, from his shirt pocket and placed it on the cut. "Hold it tight."

I pressed it on my face and felt the blood seep through its fibres. Then I realised that the same thing had happened with urine and the fibres of my pants. I had to leave. I bolted for the door, leaving behind his entreaties to stay until it was safe. I never stepped into that bookshop again.

I was in the middle of a coup, darting through streets controlled by soldiers and thugs, and all I could think of was my pee-soaked pants. I squatted every time I needed to catch a break from my mad run so no one would see the wet patches, thinking of how to get into the house, change, and take a shower without being noticed. The one sight obscure enough to briefly distract me from my pants (as I was catching my breath sheltering behind a telephone booth) was a Jeep driving by, with a few men sitting inside and a woman standing on the side—her chador looped once around her waist and fastened behind her neck—waving a wooden club in her right hand, her left hand holding the window shield as she chanted, "Long live the Shah!"

I wasn't taken to a clinic, since with all the chaos and blood no one would care about a little cut. Our neighbour, Dr. Meshakt, did the stitches for me—while I sat in a chair on her balcony smelling of sweat and urine—before she left for a double shift. When the blood was wiped off my face and my parents were reassured that I was alright, the scolding started. After the first failed coup a few days before, my father had warned me every morning that I shouldn't loiter about the city after school and come home straight away. Then I'd snuck out of school to go to a bookshop!

A couple of weeks before, I'd heard Ayatollah Entezari saying to my father that Prime Minister Mosaddegh would eventually pay for oil nationalisation. The British wouldn't settle for anything less than another concession or full compensation for the years that remained of the previous one. The Americans, on the other hand, didn't want Mosaddegh's attempts at oil nationalisation to turn into a success story of independence that could inspire other oil-rich countries. Mosaddegh was doomed, one way or another, Ayatollah Entezari had concluded. My father only sighed and shook his head.

Entezari was proved right. Before dusk, the Mosaddegh government was overthrown. The Shah returned to the country to rule with absolute power. Well, as absolute as his power could get under the gaze of Britain and America, who threatened to replace him with his son if he didn't agree to the coup.

I wasn't interested in politics yet, but I'd become connected to the coup through my wet pants and wounded face. I followed the news. Two to three hundred died during the conflicts. Mosaddegh was arrested. Later he was tried and sentenced to three years in prison for treason, which was followed by house arrest for the rest of his life.

*

I had to wait for a while before I could convince my parents that it was safe for me to go out on my own again. My random strolls around the city helped me to overcome the urge to see Forugh. It didn't always work though. One day I returned restless, and frustrated for missing mosque, and reminded myself to be more disciplined as I got ready to pray at home. I'd finished my evening prayer when I heard her name. I continued, going through different postures mechanically, so to hear more.

"Such a ridiculous title, *The Captive*!" Zari said.

"The poor girl's stuck with a handsome husband in a nice house. Somebody should save her for God's sake! Somebody! Anybody!" Zohre stopped giggling and looked at me over her huge belly. I was sitting on the prayer rug, staring at them, not pretending to pray anymore. "Are you praying or what? Don't you have anything else to do, Ismael?" She sipped her tea.

I did. I had to get my hands on the book.

*

I bought the first edition of *The Captive* nine times.

The first page read, *To my kind husband, Parviz, in appreciation of sacrifices he's made for my poetry.* I read the whole book in one sitting, with her at my side. She was longing to see *me*. She was asking *me* to hold her in my arms. In *my* kisses, she was looking for the fiery passion... I ripped the book into pieces.

Before long I was at the bookshop, buying *The Captive*, again. Then another strike of guilt and the book was lying there, torn into pieces. It didn't matter how many times I tore up the book; neither her image nor her words would leave me alone.

The seller, a middle-aged man who always wore a black waistcoat over a light brown shirt, looked at me suspiciously over his thick glasses every time I entered the bookshop. However, he was a man of a few words and never tried to engage me in any conversation. After the first few times I stopped buying other books as a cover, since it had left me with a pile of poetry books I would never read. I picked up *The Captive*, paid for it without a word, and left. I only stopped buying it when I had already memorised every single poem, word by word. All 44 of them. Now I couldn't escape it. The "Sin" was in me. I carried it around.

*

I found out who the "shameless man" was, the man depicted in "Sin" by Forugh: Nasser Khodayar, journalist and popular radio personality. He was also the writer of those supposedly fictitious pieces named "Blue Blossom" that he published in *The Intellectual*. They narrated the story of a young woman, determined to become an artist. Nasser had depicted the female persona in his stories in such a way that everybody knew it was the story of his love affair with Forugh before it went sour.

I was in my room eavesdropping when Zohre said how Forugh had sent her brother, Freidun, and a couple of her friends to persuade Nasser not to publish those stories anymore, all in vain. If you chose to be with a man like Nasser, you knew what you were getting yourself into, Zari commented. Under any other circumstances, I would have had no sympathy for the woman depicted in those stories either. She'd got what she deserved. But this wasn't any woman; this was my woman, and her honour was mine.

The day after, I heard Nasser's voice on the radio for the first time: warm, friendly, and inviting. I listened to him—indignant, furious. I punched him in the face and kicked him in the groin. He was on his knees, his bulging nose covered in blood, begging for mercy, when I heard the front door squeak open. I turned off the radio and ran for my room.

*

There was a half-finished abandoned building near our house where stray dogs sought shelter. As a result it was full of dog shit, which I used to make shit bombs. I put the shit in a thin transparent plastic bag, added some water, and used a straw to blow some air inside the plastic.

That evening, I loitered outside *The Intellectual*'s office with two freshly made shit bombs hidden in a brown paper bag. I had no plan. I had no idea about what Nasser would do after leaving the office, or even sure whether he was at work or not that day. I had only seen one picture of him, in *The Intellectual*, where he worked as an editor and I couldn't tell whether the small, black-and-white picture of his profile would be enough to recognise him from.

It was, and when he emerged from the building, I followed him from the opposite sidewalk. He was wearing a grey suit with white stripes, a black tie and a long black coat. He rolled up the collar of his coat to protect his neatly shaved cheeks against the frosty breeze. He wasn't as tall as I'd imagined, but had broad shoulders and walked with the confidence of a man who was sure of his place in the world. I shadowed him until he climbed a narrow staircase next to a carpet shop. I stood staring at the building, and in a few seconds the light of the apartment on top of the shop was turned on. What was he doing there I wondered. The apartment seemed too small to be his home, too small to fit the sense of self-importance he projected.

I sat on the curb facing the building, not knowing what I was waiting for. It was an autumn evening, but the uniform luminous clouds in the sky promised imminent snow and an early winter. I'd waited long enough for the cold to seep into my bones when a woman in a grey winter coat passed by the shop and turned upstairs. So, this is your den, you bastard! This was the place the famous Don Juan met his lovers.

Whatever happened in that apartment had inspired Forugh to write "Sin". The thought turned into a knot in my chest and pushed me to my feet. I took a bomb out. The water inside was already murky with shit. Weighing it in my right hand, I took a deep breath and squeezed the plastic gently in my hand—shaky with fear and cold—to cool my nerves. I glanced at the salesman in the carpet shop, sitting at his desk, sipping his tea, scratching his head, oblivious to the world outside.

It landed in the middle of the window and exploded. Then I acted in the most counterintuitive way. I took a few steps to the left and sat back on the curb while every cell in my body was urging me to run. I leaned back against the tree behind the curb as the brown paper bag, with another shit bomb in it, sat right next to me.

Nasser's naked torso appeared behind the window. He didn't see me. Not because I was sitting in a dark spot, but because his head was turning right and left looking for someone running as I sat right under his nose, looking at his hairy chest, feeling satisfied with the chaos I'd caused. As he turned back, he glanced at me for a second, but disregarded the teenager who was sitting on a curb, rubbing his hands together and blowing into them for warmth. The apartment's light went off and soon after he came out, turned to his left, hesitated for a second and strode off. After a while, the lady in grey stepped out, turned to her right, and walked away briskly.

A few decades later, I read an interview in which Nasser had claimed credit for Forugh's poetry. He mentioned the verse in one of her poems that read *Hey man! You turned me to a poetess* as a testimony to his claim. Reading that interview, I couldn't help but sneer remembering his anxious face on that cold autumn evening.

*

I bought the next issue of *The Intellectual*. The seventh part of "Blue Blossom" had been published. After that I punctured his car tires, parked in a small alley next to *The Intellectual's* office, and engraved it with a key on its blue hood: *Stop!*

He did not.

While looking at my most recent torn copy of *The Captive,* I came up with an idea. I was going to write Nasser a note. No one knew that I even existed, so I didn't have to be worried about my handwriting being recognised. But I was still paranoid that it might give me away, if he bothered to share a stupid letter with the police. If anything, I should've been more worried about my fingerprints. I cut out the verses *I am closing these two fiery eyes to pass through infamy* and *Don't complain of others, put an end to this madness!* from the fragmented pages of *The Captive.* I scissored out the words I needed and glued the following on a white paper: *Put an end to this infamy!* Then I took out a few more verses and words and came up with the following:

*Put an end to this infamy!*
*Aren't you afraid that eventually, this tale will drag you into the darkness of an unmarked grave? Aren't you afraid to have your name written on a dark tombstone in a silent gloomy night? Reproaching the actions, regretting the words!*

Late at night, I went to his apartment and slid the note under the door. The next and tenth part of "Blue Blossom" was the last. He may've stopped because he'd said whatever he intended to—he may've not even received my note—but I chose to believe otherwise.

\*

My father leaned his head back and closed his eyes. I looked at the old scar line on his face—hairless and raw, glimmering under the sunlight. When he trimmed his beard short the whole cut became visible. I remembered asking him about it when I was a teenager. He had run through an over-polished glass door as a kid, he'd answered. One of my attempts to learn about his past, aborted by a short answer and followed by a silence that announced the end of the conversation. I'd learnt over the years that we didn't talk to connect, only to pass on information.

I wanted to say that I thought the coup had happened before Forugh's first book was published. But I pictured him in the middle of a bookshop, a horrified teenager, urine trickling down his legs, glanced at the shopping bag between us on the bench that contained a few pieces of crumpled bread, and decided to leave the weary old man beside me to repose in peace.

*

The "Blue Blossom" may've stopped but it was already too late. Being divorced, having no source of income and living in the house of a raging father, whose shoulders couldn't carry the shame of a divorcee daughter who was now the main character of an obscene story too, pushed her over the edge. She had a nervous breakdown, attempted suicide, and was admitted to Rezaei Psychiatric Hospital where she went through electroconvulsive therapy.

"Once a crazy bitch, always a crazy bitch," I heard people whisper.

Crazy or not, I couldn't wait to see her. In my free time I hung around the street, sitting on a curb or leaning against a tree with a crime novel in my hand, hoping to catch a glimpse of her.

One day, absorbed in my book, I didn't notice that she was standing a few metres away from me. I raised my head and she was there. She wore a long red T-shirt, white pyjama bottoms and black slippers. Her hair was tangled and scruffy. She looked bewildered, putting her hand on a tree as if trying to keep her balance, staring at a point on the ground. She snapped out of it and murmured something unintelligible before looking at an envelope in her right hand next to her wallet as if wondering why it was there. She took a step forward towards me. I wanted to stand up and run but I couldn't move.

"Would you post this for me?"

I nodded. She opened her wallet to pay me for the favour.

"No need," I whispered. She mumbled what I assumed to be words of appreciation. My eyes followed her as she walked back slowly towards her father's house, took out the key from her wallet, and disappeared behind the door.

The envelope was addressed to her ex-husband, Parviz, in Ahvaz. I held it up under the sun, hoping the rays of light travelling through would reveal some of the words. Nothing. On the one hand, I was dying to know its content and thought of finding a way to open it without leaving any trace. If I posted it in a day or two, she would never find out. On the other hand, I didn't want to ruin the satisfaction I felt at being trusted by her. I posted the letter as it was.

Having seen Forugh in that condition was an uncanny experience. As a teenager, when you love someone, you place them beyond the ordinary and mundane, and to see them so fragile, so human, comes as a shock. However, even that unsettling experience didn't stifle my urge to see her. Not even for a full day. The day after, when I returned from school, I devoured my lunch—not listening to my mother saying that gulping my food was bad for my digestion—grabbed a book and sat under the shade of the robust plane tree in front of our house.

Waiting for her to pass by.

I could never imagine that four decades later when her letters to Parviz were published I would read them, wondering which one of those letters, if any, I'd held in my hand that late afternoon. Was it the letter in which she asked Parviz for financial support to arrange a trip to Europe? She told him that if she wanted to go, it wasn't because visiting other lands was of any interest to her. No. She believed that under this sky, one would never face anything new, and the core of life was vanity and endless repetition, and there was no real asylum in this world for her restless soul. Or perhaps the one she wrote to complain to Parviz of moments of oblivion when her mind got emptied of any thought (had I witnessed one of those moments?) and she felt like she wasn't Forugh anymore, but someone who had lost her name, someone who suffered from understanding the absurdity of life and existence.

I could never be sure, since most of the letters weren't dated. Understandably, she assumed she was writing to her ex-husband and not to the generations of her fans to come, those who would be trying to make sense of the life of an "iconoclast" who became an icon.

*

I was reading a book under the shade of the plane tree, as was my daily ritual, when the door of the Farrokhzads' house opened. Mrs. Farrokhzad appeared, holding a tray that carried a bowl of water and a Quran. I knew straightaway that someone was travelling. She was followed by Mr. Farrokhzad, Forugh, Forugh'son Kami and her brother Freidun, who placed a suitcase at the back of a ragtop Jeep before getting behind its wheel. I walked towards Hasan's house and put my hand on the bell without pressing it. Now I was only a few metres away.

Mrs. Farrokhzad put the tray down and embraced Forugh. She sniffed into her tissue, got on her knees, squeezed Kami in her embrace and kissed him a few times. She stood up right in front of her father, whose eyes were glittering with tears that he blinked away. They stared at each other for a second or two, without uttering a word.

Mrs. Farrokhzad held the Quran up and Forugh passed underneath it; then she poured the water on the ground as Forugh walked towards the car. The engine roared. I collected all my courage and waved as the car passed by. She didn't notice me.

"What's up?" I heard Hasan's voice. He was standing behind me. I had buzzed the bell at some point.

"Do you want to hang out?" I asked.

At the time I didn't know that Forugh was travelling to Europe and wouldn't return for the next fourteen months.

\*

Her second collection, *The Wall*, was published soon after. *To Parviz, for what we shared in the past, and with the hope that this small token shows my appreciation for his kindness*, read the first page. Lying under the sun, on a green patch in a park, I read every poem, but it was after reading these verses that a peace took me over:

> *You don't make me feel warm anymore,*
> *oh love, you frozen sun,*
> *my heart is a wilderness of despair*
> *I'm tired, tired even of love.*
> *The blossom of your passion withered too,*
> *oh poetry, you enchanting devil*
> *finally, my soul was awakened,*
> *awakened from this painful dream.*

She'd realised that she was pursuing and sacrificing herself for nothing but an illusion. Art, poetry, love, living one's life and dreams, were only words: slight and weightless. Loneliness, depression, poverty and pain were the reality: hefty and crushing. What else did you expect? I thought.

That night, I went to the abandoned house, the one that was a shelter for stray dogs. I ripped out the pages of the introduction that quoted "Sura Al-Qamar" from the Quran, folded them, kissed them, and put them in my pocket. Then I made a small fire in a pit and tore the rest of the book apart, feeding it page by page to the fire as I recited the whole *Sura* under my breath:

*The Last Hour draws near, and the moon is split asunder! But if they were to see a sign, they would turn aside and say, "An ever-recurring delusion!"— for they are bent on giving it the lie, being always want to follow their own desires... But nay—the Last Hour is the time when they shall truly meet their fate; and that Last Hour will be most calamitous, and most bitter... Behold, the God-conscious will find themselves in gardens and running waters, in a seat of truth, in the presence of a Sovereign who determines all things...*

I watched every page turn into ashes, every word into smoke. There was no doubt, no question. My body was calm. My mind clear. Oblivious to the howling of the beasts.

*

The sun was setting and it was time to go home. As we left the park, my father grabbed my hand with an unexpectedly strong grip, holding to it as if he relied on me to keep him going. I took a glance at his right hand enfolding my left, the same hand that had held a letter of Forugh's.

As a fan of her works, I'd read the collection of her letters to Parviz years before I left Iran. The bit I still remembered was part of a letter written before their marriage. She said how disinterested she was in money, how a simple life by his side was enough for her, and how she was going to keep the cost of their wedding affordable. There was something hopeful and naive about the letter—written by a sixteen-year-old girl in love—that I found beautifully sad. Nothing like her late poems—written by a disillusioned woman who had experienced life beyond her years—which I always found sadly beautiful.

"What do you want to have for dinner?" I asked when we reached home. He didn't feel like eating and went straight to bed.

# Chapter Three

Last night I thought of cancelling my morning classes, but my father insisted that I should continue with my life as if he wasn't around. After two hours of teaching I came back to make lunch. The apartment was empty. Where has he gone? He didn't know his way around and barely spoke any English. Why doesn't he carry a mobile? He might have gone to the nearby convenience store.

The salesperson at the shop remembered him, as he'd found his jumper peculiar for such warm weather. He'd also bought a small packet of bread and paid for it with a hundred-dollar note. I rushed towards my unit. He must've gone this way and taken a wrong turn somewhere. He was nowhere around and I started looking for him in the opposite direction. Passing by the convenience store, I took the first turn. Further down the road, he was standing near a bookshop, dazed, sweat running down his forehead. Something came up from my chest and turned to a lump in my throat. I swallowed it back and ran towards him.

"Baba jan! Where have you been? I was worried sick!"

He let me hug him before saying, "I just came to buy some bread."

His hands were empty.

"It's too hot. Let's go home."

We returned home using every bit of shade we could find. I passed him a bottle of water. He gulped it down, water dripping down his sparse beard, running down his neck.

"Now, you need to change your clothes," I said. He wore a short-sleeved undershirt under his grey jumper. It was soaked in sweat. "Leave the white one for me to wash."

I put after-sun lotion on the burning spots. A bit on his forehead and cheeks, some on his neck and shoulders, and some on the sweat rashes on his back. He let me rub the remedy into his skin. It sucked in the cream like sunbaked land taking in water.

"You should take a shower. I'll put more lotion on when you're done."

After the shower, he sat on the edge of the bed and drank the iced tea I'd made for him. He slurped the last drops, keeping the ice cubes back with the tea spoon, and placed the glass on the bedside table. He leaned back, ran his palms up and down his thighs and exhaled. Something about his face told me that he was about to continue with his story.

"Why don't we just take some rest today, and when the weather has cooled off, I'll take you to the Botanic Gardens. You'll like it." I sat back on the sofa.

He took his feet off the ground, sat cross-legged on the bed, and covered his lower body under the bedsheet. "I'm alright. I don't have much time left."

What did he mean by that, I wondered. Now, in Adelaide? Or ever?

*

It was during Forugh's absence that God completely conquered me. He rooted in me and grew out of me with my scraggy beard. He closed my eyelids when I saw an alluring woman, blocked my ears at the presence of any obscene words, and flew out of my mouth riding righteous words.

Everyday I worked as a volunteer to clean and prepare the mosque before everybody came in. After the congregational prayers, when everyone left, I would stay and talk with Entezari about the sharia, or ask questions if I had any. One day, when I was asking whether God would find it in his grace to forgive us even when we repent but give into temptation again, I burst into tears.

"It's alright, my son! We're not infallible like the Prophet and his grace-ful family. Remember that your body is instrumental in any sin and make it tired through productive physical activities. And learn to control your eyes, as whatever your eyes see your heart fancies. Tomorrow I'll bring you something. It was a gift from my father. It helped me to discipline my body and by God's will it will help you too."

It was a small knife. A switchblade not more than five centimetres long. Dull and old, it could cut nothing. I pressed the blade to my palm to distract myself whenever I had a forbidden thought or urge. I carried it everywhere. It reassured me whenever I held it in my hand or touched it in my pocket. After a while, my skin grew red and swollen from the constant pressure. It didn't do enough though. At the end of the day, that tiny knife was no weapon to fight such a great war—a holy war.

*

During Ramadan, Entezari invited me over to his house to break my fast. After the evening prayers, we left for his house near the mosque, where he lived with his wife and four daughters.

"My youngest has Down's syndrome," Entezari said.

"I'm sorry," I mumbled.

"At first, I was heartbroken." He thought he'd been punished for not being thankful for the three healthy daughters God had blessed him with. For insisting on having a son, ignorant of the fact that even the Prophet, peace be upon him, had only one daughter, Fatima, and she brought him more blessing than any son could do. "But it's all good now and I feel blessed having her in my life."

"She is lucky to have you as her father."

"You're like the son I've never had," he smiled.

It was because of the feeling of intimacy born at that moment that I asked him about his past life.

"The story of my life doesn't matter, my son," he said. "Talking about yourself is not only pointless, but it also harms the process of your spiritual cultivation."

We stopped in front of a low-ceiling house made of old reddish clay bricks; its white door covered in patches of rust wherever the paint had peeled off. Inside, a white sheet was separating the small entrance from the living room. "*Yaallah*," Entezari announced our presence as we took our shoes off and placed them on a shoe rack. He hesitated for a moment to ensure the women of the house were decent before he pulled the sheet aside and we entered the living room. The only furnitures were a *galim* spread in the middle and two *poshtis* sitting against the wall, all pieces red with the same recurring black motif of an eye.

The room, where we sat on a carpet around the *sofreh,* had no furniture except for a *poshti* placed behind a small desk where one could sit cross-legged and study. I was impressed with the shelves of books that surrounded the room. In our house the only reading materials were the *Quran, Simplified Stories of Shahnameh,* a *Diwan of Hafez,* my collection of poorly crafted crime novels, some poetry books, and a bunch of magazines my sisters bought that I wasn't allowed to touch, which I did anyway.

The dinner was simple. Bread, cheese, walnuts, fresh vegetables and barley soup. We ate in silence. When I was finished, the imam's wife teased me with a smile, "Have more, my son. Are you on a diet?"

I thanked her and politely refused. I was in one of those phases when I tried to discipline my body by not feeding it too much. Mrs Entezari and three of her daughters—wearing the same grey chadors printed with small white petals—collected the *sofreh* and dirty dishes and left the room. Entezari's youngest daughter sat on his lap, put her hands around his neck, and leaned her face against his shoulder. He kissed her cheek and whispered something into her ear. She left, her chador hanging from her shoulders and exposing her curly black hair, waving at me with a smile. Entezari guessed that I was about to ask him another question and said, "No more talk about sharia tonight. I'm sure you know enough to survive another day."

We chatted about my family, my school, and my future plans. My father wanted me to become a physician. He believed it to be the most rewarding career one could have.

"He's right, your father. It is a blessing to reduce your brothers' and sisters' suffering. What about the shop then?"

"He plans to rent it out when he retires. But I'm not sure what I want to do yet."

"You'll find your way."

Entezari was relatively young yet had already managed to reach the rank of ayatollah, which made his choice of being the imam of a suburban mosque in Tehran a bit of a mystery. "Can I ask why you chose to work here?"

"The only way I could stay true to myself and my beliefs was to leave the Qom Seminary and become financially independent," he said. The dominant belief in the seminary was that philosophy was the mother of heresy. Moreover, the high-ranked clergy followed the doctrine of non-political Islam. That had put him in a difficult position. In this self-imposed exile, he could focus on writing on political Islam, as was his lifelong ambition. He let me go through his notes. I found the jargon difficult to comprehend and lost interest quickly.

At one point, I asked him if I could browse his library. I leafed through a few books before I picked *The Republic* from a pile of books at a corner near the study table.

"That's a really interesting book," he said. "Would you like to borrow it?"

That night my long-lasting obsession with Plato started. I was fascinated with the concept of utopia formalised by Plato and above all with the notion of the philosopher king—the rule of the wisest.

The day I finished reading *The Republic* for the first time, I felt so excited that I went straight to Entezari's house, even though it was late for a visit. When he opened the door, I said that I'd come to return the book. He sensed that I was eager to talk and asked me to come in with a smile.

Entezari considered Plato to be one of the most religious people who had ever lived, in the true sense of the word. For instance, what Plato said about "the vision of the form of the good" was nothing but a religious experience; a kind of knowledge one could achieve intuitively, but couldn't communicate clearly or fully. It was similar to Islamic mysticism when one experienced God's cosmic presence. Great mystics had tried to convey the experience through poetry, but words were always too limited, too feeble, to contain such magnificent encounters.

"I haven't thought of Plato that way," I said as I skimmed through *The Republic*, as if doing that could help me to get the point I'd missed.

Entezari found Plato to be very compatible with his Islamic worldview too. "For instance, consider his idea about the guardian," he said. The Prophet, peace be upon him, and the twelve infallible Imams worked as good examples of Islamic guardians. What he admired about Plato was that he gave the idea of the guardian and the rule of the wisest a rational ground. We were Muslims and our wisest, besides all other necessary traits, must've had mastery of Islam. So during the time of the Hidden Imam, the guardian must be a *faqih*.

"And what are ordinary people like me expected to do?" I asked and put *The Republic* on his desk.

"You can keep the book." He slid the book back towards me. "In a society ruled by the *faqih*, if everyone performs their duty they'll reach unity; the biggest disaster a society can face is disunity."

I still wanted to chat. But I knew that the imam was a man of habit who followed a strict routine. I said goodbye and left.

*

With Forugh away, I was absorbed by the imam's words. During our talks and discussions, I experienced the feeling that was the highest reward of any intellectual endeavour, an ephemeral and intense experience that kept me coming back for more: *joy.*

Forugh (turned into a blurry figure) was nothing but the name of an old longing now. I yearned for women of course, it was only natural, and even I knew that, but my desire was fluid with no direction, no fixed object to attach itself to it, and therefore it lost some of its vigour. What I yearned for now, was to be a man of piety and wisdom like Entezari.

That was my will and my body had to yield to it.

I'd introduced elements of an ascetic life to my daily routines. Instead of sleeping on a mattress, I was sleeping on a thin *doshak* for only few hours a night. I woke up at midnight to pray and read Quran, before going to mosque for the morning prayer. I stopped eating while still hungry, had the simplest food (only what the poorest could afford), and fasted on Fridays. I spent most my time on reading philosophy and mystic poetry, interpreting the Quran and other religious texts. My father was growing concerned. "It's good that you care about your religion, but everything in moderation, my son," he kept telling me, and I kept ignoring him.

One day when I was waiting at the mosque entrance to go back to Entezari's house, he told me it would be better if I spent more time on my own study and gave my father a hand at the shop. I knew straight away that my father had spoken to him.

"Sure, I will," I said.

I went back home and raised hell. I was shouting at the top of my lungs, telling my father that if he didn't want to encourage me to grow intellectually and spiritually, at least he shouldn't stop me. I concluded my little speech by telling him that he didn't know much about the true Islam.

"I know this much, that in the Quran we're asked to respect our parents right after we're asked to worship Allah," he said without raising his voice. He had got me. I had nothing to say and went back to my room mumbling under my breath.

After that, I began seeing Entezari less often, but I didn't change my routine. I felt so transformed that I thought the curse had left. My body wasn't much of a burden anymore. It was light, disciplined, and I felt strong in its weakness.

Then Forugh returned from her trip, and so did my restlessness.

*

She soon moved out of her father's house to share an apartment with a girl-friend. Back then, two single women living together was unconventional enough to get people talking. After learning of her whereabouts, I hung around the area, in bookshops, cafés, and parks.

One day, tired of my aimless strolls, I was lying on a small patch of green in front of the local library, reading *The Republic* again. I carried it around as a way of defying the voice in my head that shamed me for believing in the importance of knowledge and discipline and then wasting my time loitering about, desperate for a glance of a woman.

That day, I was reading the segment on how art must serve the social order, and based on that argument I was evaluating Forugh's poetry—those poems that I could recite word by word—as worthless when I saw her on the opposite side of the street. Her silky purple skirt proved that all those feelings of ascendency and control were nothing but a delusion that faded with every step I took to follow her. She entered a café and sat at a table for two. I stayed across the street, where I could see her profile. She put her handbag on the table, had a brief chat with the waiter, and sat staring straight ahead.

Parviz entered the café shortly after and sat across from her. Their body gestures grew tenser as they talked their way into a quarrel. Were they arguing over their son? That seemed the most plausible explanation. Forugh had left him with her mother-in-law before her trip to Europe, and now she refused to let her see him: the only time that I'd heard my mother disagree with my sisters, who thought Forugh was too "unstable" to be trusted with raising a kid. "She's still a mother and shouldn't be kicked out of her kid's life," my mother had said.

Forugh thumped the table with her fist; Parviz pushed his chair back, got on his feet, hesitated to say something as he threw some money on the table, and left. As Parviz strode away, she said something back, lowered her head, and placed her forehead on her fists.

I wanted to linger, to see what she did next, but I realised that I didn't have *The Republic* with me. I could always buy another copy, but this was Entezari's gift. I darted back and found it next to the tree where I'd been reading under its shade. By the time I reached the café again, sweating and panting for breath, she was already gone.

While Forugh travelled in Europe, her third collection, *Rebellion,* had been published. I'd promised myself not to read it. But that day, I walked from the café to a nearby bookshop and bought it. I sat on a bench outside the shop and didn't move until I finished it.

In the poems of the collection she'd questioned God's justice and pictured Satan as a servant who had no choice but to fulfil his obscene role. I found the whimsical and at times wicked God was portrayed in a manner offensive to my beliefs. It was after reading that collection that I tried to write poetry that would represent the true face of God. The Almighty, The Just, and The Merciful.

After a few months, I didn't need a second opinion to know that I'd failed. However, unable to acknowledge my literary incompetence, I continued writing poems, which were nothing but third-rate copies of great classics. My failure in creating any decent poetry added another feeling to the peculiar collection of sentiments I had for her: jealousy.

*

I saw her again on one of those nights that I couldn't sleep—my skin insufferably alert. Staring at the ceiling in the dark, my body was strangling my soul, and nothing—prayers, poetry, mental games—could weaken its grasp. I got out of bed and tiptoed out of the house. A still night. Clear sky. The city was asleep, ignorant of my anxious steps and restive mind.

I was scurrying by the alley behind our street—the one with Forugh's in-laws' house in it— when I saw a silhouette leaning against a wall, dimly lit by the streetlamp. I turned into the alley and as I got closer the blurry figure turned out to be Forugh. Her face was ruddy, and her hair, half tied, half loose, had settled on her left cheek. Her left hand in her lap and her right was on the ground holding a half-drunk bottle of vodka. She raised her head, looked at me, took another sip, and murmured a few incomprehensible words. I started counting in my head to cool my nerves when she let go of the bottle—the sound of its landing pierced the silent night and startled me—and raised her right hand towards me. I stared at her hand hanging in the air, waiting for me to grab it and pull her onto her feet. A shiver took over my body. I turned and ran. I should go to her parents, I thought. They'll know what to do. Before turning out of the alley, I took one final glance over my shoulder. She was lying on the ground now, her thighs drawn up to her torso, her face resting on her arm.

I stood in front of her parents' house. A mixture of fear and shame stopped me from knocking on the door. I went back home and lay in bed, unable to get rid of the image of the trembling hand hanging in the air, and soon it wasn't asking for help anymore but pointing at me, accusing me of being a coward.

*

"I'm a bit tired, let's continue tomorrow."

"Why are you telling me all this?" I asked.

He held my gaze for a moment. "Because I must," he whispered and averted his gaze.

"You must?"

"Just be patient with me, my son."

Do I have a choice when this may be the last time I see you? But perhaps in return you can be patient with me and listen to a little story of mine? About my first kiss? First time I had sex? Or first time I tried alcohol? Actually, that's a good one. Vodka in a can. Whatever it was, Payam's "guy" sold it to us as vodka. Best Russian vodka. He would be driving a white Peugeot 504, he'd told Payam. There was a white Peugeot parked in a corner, but that couldn't be him. A lady with a baby in her arms was in the front seat. Only when we couldn't wait any longer we approached the car and Payam knocked at the window cautiously. The driver opened the boot and passed Payam a plastic bag. What was going on? Payam asked referring to the lady. His family. He brought them along so nobody would get suspicious. And still he couldn't be more obvious, Payam raised the black plastic bag and smiled. We got hammered, just like Forugh. Unlike her, we could have been arrested, whipped, and expelled from the university. There is probably still

40

a vomit stain on the carpet of the room 303 of my university dormitory.

"I talked to Ellie this morning. She said she can't wait to meet you." I said.

He nodded before asking, "Are you two planning to get married?"

"We haven't planned anything yet, but I think so."

"I've always respected your choices—even when I didn't approve of them. I said nothing when you stopped praying and fasting, when you decided to leave the country; even now, I rather understand your decision on not eating meat. But now you might marry someone with whom you cannot communicate in your own language. Sometimes I wonder how much…"

He paused and I completed his sentence for him. "How much of my heritage is left in me? How much of my identity?" He kept quiet. "There is no such a thing as a uniform identity. And it's just too complex to be reduced to a few romantic notions—"

"I understand, my son. At least, I'm trying to. Now I need to close my eyes for a bit."

"You comment on my relationship when you've never even bothered to ask why I like her?" I looked into his eyes demanding him to ask the question before I would continue.

"Why do you like her, my son?"

"Because she doesn't 'need' me. She wants me in her life because I can have meaningful conversations with her and make her laugh with my 'dark' humour. She is free to do whatever she wants to do and is financially independent and she's not looking for a man as her ticket to more freedom or more money. And don't look at me like that, I'm aware that I'm oversimplifying, that relationships are more complicated than that, that every society has its own way to control and discipline people, but I'm trying to make a point here which I hope you'll get."

"It's all good, my son. I always wished for your happiness."

"Of course you did, why else would you call me Saeed—the blessed one?" I walked to the cabinets, took a small sack of potatoes out and threw a few in the sink. "Are you still writing poetry?" I asked to finally break the tension.

"I haven't written a single word in years. I chose not to be a phoney poet, which ultimately turned to be my best achievement when it comes to poetry."

*

I left for work earlier than I needed to. I was relieved to be out of the house. After everything I'd heard, I felt comfortable around my father only when he talked; when there was no silence to give rise to questions and uneasy thoughts.

I had mixed feelings. There were moments I thought my father had no right to appear, unfold all these stories to unburden himself, and disappear again, when we'd never had this tradition of talking about our personal affairs or feelings. We'd never talked about adolescence or sex. He was breaking a thirty-five-year-old agreement based on silence and denial: no talking when it came to desires. At the same time, I couldn't wait to hear more. To see more of this new face forming in front of me, coming out of the shadows, no matter how uncomfortable the whole process made me.

While teaching, I made all sorts of mistakes until my student asked whether I was alright or not. I finished my session, but didn't return home straightaway. I walked to a café and ordered a pot of ginger tea. I picked the novel *Disgrace* out of my backpack to read, but soon after opened my laptop. I read the first page of the short story I was working on. Unable to focus, I skimmed through the rest, my eyes skipped down random words, random sentences, with nothing to hang on into. I sat there staring at the blinking cursor on the screen. Then I shut my laptop and called Ellie. She asked if I was having a good time with my father. I asked how her work was. She talked, complained, and I happily listened.

"Would you tell me something you've never told anyone else?" I asked finally. (Wasn't it why I had called her in the first place?)

"What do you mean?"

"I mean something you've kept to yourself all these years. Would you share it with me?"

"I don't know if I have such a thing to start with."

"Of course you have. Everybody has."

"Maybe we could talk about it later?"

"I miss you," I said after a pause.

"Miss you too, babe. And that was such an endearing picture of you and your dad, send me more."

I had got only the one so far. "Sure. I will," I said.

"By the way, was that a pimple on your nose?"

"Yeah."

"The cream I got for you, must be still in your fridge. And I really like the new ending you've sent me." She was referring to the story I had finished long ago. I had rewritten the ending many times; none she had found compelling enough. "I think this is it."

I ambled around the city and bought some groceries that I didn't need. I considered going to a cinema, but decided against it. I couldn't leave my father alone until midnight. When I reached home it wasn't even 9:00pm, but he was already in bed. That was a relief. Trying not to make any noise, I lay down on the sofa.

# Chapter Four

The first scene that came into focus when I opened my eyes, was my father sitting on the balcony, a cup of tea at his side and the *Diwan of Hafez* in his right hand. I'd dreamt nonstop. I could only recall bits and pieces of the dreams, but they were so intense that they'd left me exhausted. We didn't say much during the morning, except that I asked him how he wanted his eggs, and tea, black or green? Afterwards I walked around the apartment doing unnecessary chores, waiting for him to continue with his story. He felt my impatience and said, "I need to go for a stroll and clear my head. Do you have any teaching today?"

"No."

"Maybe we can go to the Botanic Gardens that you told me about."

I packed some food and we left.

"Do you like it here?" he asked me on the way.

"I don't hate it," I said. "I've learnt a lot about myself that I wouldn't have otherwise. After a year or so, I realised that I'd become so addicted to depression and anxiety that I looked down at people and the carefree 'little' lives they led here. Only after meeting Ellie did I start learning to respect my body and its needs and to enjoy the little things in life. Only then did I realise that one could have a meaningful life without being crushed by it."

"But are you happy?"

"I'm trying to be content knowing that beating one's destiny requires a lot of hard work and discipline, and even then it's a good chance you'd fail."

"Maybe you were meant to leave."

"What do you mean?"

"When you were trying to get your military exemption I hoped that you couldn't."

"Really?" I stopped and turned to him. His words had startled me. "Even though I felt miserable and was desperate to leave?"

"I thought if you didn't get exempted, after two years of military service you'd forget about leaving altogether," he said, and continued to walk.

"You were rooting for me not to get exempted! Even though you told me once that you *truly* despised your own military service? What happened to 'All that matters is your happiness'?"

"If you were a parent, you'd understand."

"I don't think it'd make any difference."

"It would, take my word for it. Anyway, I have much better reasons than military service to loathe that period of my life."

*

A couple of months before I was about to enlist for military service, Vahid, my father's cousin, came to stay with us. My father let him stay in the yellow-brick unit we had in our yard—which was nothing more than a room with a tiny kitchen, and a bathroom attached to it—until he could secure a job and get on his feet. My mother didn't like the idea. My father didn't want to hear about it.

Vahid was six feet tall with broad shoulders, and his unexpectedly sea-blue eyes stood out next to his dark skin and inky black hair. He would've been considered classically handsome if not for his legs, disproportionately short for his height, and his small hands with stubby fingers. A recent graduate from a French university, everything about him was different—the way he talked, carried himself, and even held his cigarettes—and because of that, I was both drawn to and intimidated by him. It took me a while before I could collect all my courage and knock on his door. He was sitting at his table. A book in a foreign language was open in front of him.

"I wanted to say hi."

"*Génial!* It can get quite lonely here."

We talked about his time abroad. What did he like most about France? How was the weather? Were people friendly? How was the university?

What was sociology about? Was it true that at first he was supposed to study medicine?

"That was the plan," he said. His father had sponsored him to study medicine in France, but when he had found out that for all these years Vahid had been studying sociology instead he cut his funding. Vahid worked in a restaurant to finance himself and got his master's degree. He received a scholarship to do his Ph.D. but he decided to come back. He could be more useful in his own country, he believed.

I wanted to bring up Forugh's name as casually as possible. I had come to his room to learn if he'd read her poetry—what he thought about it, and about her. But I was afraid that if I uttered her name something in my eyes, an uncontrollable jerk of a muscle in my face, would reveal my secret. Moreover, listening to him talk so eloquently, using words I didn't even know the meaning of, I was afraid to look stupid talking about the poetry of a poet almost no one took seriously.

I also had another reason to be there. Reading the books I was borrowing from Entezari had awakened a thirst in me. I was restless to learn and, more importantly, to prove—to myself more than anyone else—that my religious worldview was superior to all others. How many well-educated people, with a degree from an excellent university in Europe, did I know? Nothing could be as reassuring as the approval of someone like him.

"Don't you think returning to our Islamic roots could solve our social issues?" I asked at some point. He knew that the idea had its own supporters, but he found it naive.

"You're a Muslim, right?" I asked.

"I don't consider myself one."

"But you believe in God?"

"Nah. I believe in human beings! In flesh and blood! And in their suffering!"

I couldn't say anything. It was like a punch that knocked all of the words out of my mouth.

For a while, I found it difficult to face Vahid again. Not because he was against everything I believed in, but because he'd expressed it so nonchalantly. No question, no argument, no doubt, nothing but a cold-hearted "no". He'd noticed my disappointment in him, as one day when he saw me in the yard, he said straightaway, "I'm not a believer myself. But I think that some new religious interpretation might help the process of modernisation in Iran. Do you want to come over for a cup of tea?"

I was about to leave the house for the evening prayers at the mosque. "Yes," I said anyway. I would pray later at home. The mere fact that he'd tried to make me feel better meant a lot to me.

From that day onward I saw him more often. I mostly listened to him talk without uttering a word, as I was intimidated into silence by his apparent intellect. What was a Hegelian take on history? How was it different from Marx's? Who was Schopenhauer? How could I be "will to power" and nothing else? What did that even mean? Was morality relative? What was Special Relativity? It sounded too complicated, but I needed to understand it. Vahid believed that Special Relativity pointed towards moral relativism—an idea I found utterly unacceptable—and I required a good understanding of both theories to defend my stance. There was no end to either my questions or my confusion.

One night when he was talking about a French poet, I seized the opportunity and asked, as casually as possible, whether he'd read any of Forugh's works. He'd read a couple and he'd even met her a few times at Café Naderi where he hung out with his friends on Thursdays. "Have you been there? It's one of the first modern cafés in Tehran, built by an Armenian immigrant who—"

"What did you talk to her about?" I asked.

"There are so many great poets, both classic and contemporary. Why are you interested in her?"

"I have no interest in her!" I rushed to say. "I've heard people talking about her work, and I am wondering what all the fuss is about?"

Vahid believed that people talked about her poetry because its topics were controversial, because as naive as she was, she'd chosen to appear naked in front of the reader. In terms of concept and form she had nothing to offer though. "Did you know she was using *iconoclast* as her pseudonym when she'd just started writing poetry? The ego behind that choice!"

I kept quiet. I didn't know what ego meant.

"Don't get me wrong," Vahid continued. He was all for women's empowerment. He admired nothing more than an independent woman and had been in love with one once. However, women like Forugh were nothing but westernised dolls. They had neither the purity of our mothers nor the intelligence of the modern women in the west. Full of contradiction and confusion.

"You were in love?" I asked. "With whom?"

"You only got that from all I said?" he said with a smile.

"I was just curious. Sorry."

"Don't be. Nothing's worth our curiosity more than love. She was a French girl in my class. I asked her out and she said no. And about Forugh's poetry. I'm going to tell you something that I haven't shared with anyone before."

He slept with a woman for the first time when he'd just moved to France. She was a prostitute. After she left, he woke up in the middle of the night with her body odour in his nose. It was not only on his body. The room was filled with it. He opened the window. The cold air rushed in. He waited until he was shivering but the smell was still there. He ran into the bathroom and rubbed his skin for an hour or so before he was convinced that the smell was gone. The day after, he had a fever. He recovered quickly from the cold but the gloom stayed with him for a while. There was something sad about her, about the way she counted the money, about her scarlet cheeks, about how she said he could call her any time, that he was a gentleman, about the fact that he couldn't bring himself to say a nice word to her and couldn't wait for her to leave.

"You know, if that prostitute wanted to write poetry it'd turn out like Forugh's." He lit a cigarette, took a long drag, and looked at me. "That's how I feel about her poetry."

One Thursday, I collected all my courage and asked Vahid if I could join him and his friends at Café Naderi.

"Sure, but it's at sunset," he smirked.

I was going to miss the early congregational prayers if I joined them. "It's alright," I said, and averted my gaze.

Café Naderi was a two-story building with a small brick facade and a white balustrade on the edge of its roof. Its wooden door was set within a round-headed arch, and the space within the arch above the door carried its name. A similar arch-and-door structure was replicated on the second floor which led to a small balcony with metal fences facing the street. The building had two large square windows next to its entrance, and four casement wooden windows within gothic frames at the top. The first floor functioned as a café and confectionary and led to large back garden while the second floor was a hostel.

Vahid introduced me to the group of people sitting around a table next to a white sculpture of an angel holding a vase on her shoulder. Forugh wasn't among them. She might show up later, I thought. She did not. Despite my first disappointing experience, I attended those meetings every Thursday. I wasn't interested in their discussions. Most of them were inclined towards leftist ideas that I had no sympathy for; some of them had even been active members of the communist Tudeh Party before it was dissolved by the Shah. They mostly talked about contemporary politics, and at times, literature and arts. I'd started thinking that the whole thing was just a waste of time when I finally met Forugh.

One of the people who frequented the café was Nader Naderpur, a respected contemporary poet. Vahid knew him from his time in France when Nader was doing a bachelor's degree in French literature. That day Nader had finished reading one of his latest poems when he suddenly collected his stuff to leave. Vahid turned and looked at the entrance. I did the same.

Forugh was coming in, at her side a man I'd never seen before.

"You can't leave whenever she appears," Vahid whispered.

"I have dinner with my *fiancée*, and I'm already late," Nader said.

Forugh arrived at the table. "Are you going to wash your hands, Nader? Eat once with your hands unwashed, something good may come out of it," she said with a grin. Nader ignored her comment and left.

"How's the great poet doing?" Vahid asked Forugh.

"Well, I know you're being sarcastic, and I don't care. I'm not a great poet, but I still take poetry as a serious business."

"Then how come nothing that really matters is reflected in this serious business of yours?" Vahid asked. He glanced around the table wearing a smirk, as if waiting for a round of applause.

"I only write about things that I know. I cannot fake interest in something just because it's the fashion of the day. No real artist should do that!"

"Nima is your favourite poet, right? But—"

"I like him because he's genuine," Forugh interjected. "When I read him I feel like I am dealing with a human being, not a collection of superficial emotions or ideas. There is complexity behind his apparent simplicity, and all the important and dark questions of life are reflected in his poetry."

"But he was a very socially conscious poet. I personally don't see that in your poetry," Vahid said as he slurped his tea.

"The whole process of creation must be organic," Forugh answered. "There are good poets who write about the important issues of the day, but they don't sound genuine. They are passionate about those topics, but have no real understanding of the themes of their creations. You can't write about something just because you're fond of it."

"You have to accept that—"

"Let me finish!" she raised her voice. "There are other poets, some of them very talented, who write just to be praised—one of them just left—and this will ruin them in the long run. A poet shouldn't care about what her audience or critics think when she writes poetry, but should drag them along as she grows."

"Wait a minute here," Vahid said, agitated, his smirk long gone. "So an artist shouldn't care about what's happening around him?"

The discussion went on for another hour. I sat there in silence, looking at her talking about poetry as if her life depended on it, memorising every detail of her face, every hand gesture, every tiny movement.

"*Putain*," Vahid said on the way back.

"Who was the man sitting next to Forugh?"

Vahid stopped for a second to light a cigarette. "One of her lovers, I guess."

"What's Nader's business with Forugh?"

"Nader dated her for a while." He had a family farm near Tehran where he, Vahid and Forugh hung out. More often than not, Forugh read her poems to Nader and he corrected them for her. Nader was the one who had turned some of her poems into something readable. "I'm happy for Nader. He's getting married soon."

"Why did they break up?"

"Not sure. I just know that he dodged a bullet there. Have you read any of his poetry? It's quite good. Not like Forugh's, the gist of which is using sex for fame."

Vahid started citing one of Nader's poems called "The old sculptor". I was just nodding my head without paying any attention when he suddenly said, "Why do you like her anyway?" His smirk was not the usual one, this time it was crooked and sulky.

"Who?"

"Forugh! Who else?" he said condescendingly.

"I don't like her!"

"*Allez*! It was so obvious, the way you were looking at her and all." He crushed his cigarette butt on a tree trunk and let it fall.

"I don't know what you are talking about," I said. "I'm going to the mosque." We were passing by a mosque I'd never been to. The time for congregational prayer had passed, but I could still pray alone and get rid of Vahid.

I stopped going to his Thursday meetings.

*

For another month, though, I still visited the café. I always ordered a cup of tea and read a book seated at a small table, almost hidden behind the counter—my senses engaged in looking for any trace of her.

During one of those random visits to the café, I saw Nader sitting alone at a table, and every now and then jotting a few words on a notebook. To reach my usual spot, I passed behind him, trying not to attract his attention. Forugh's last collection, *Rebellion,* was on top of the pile of books in front of him. The waiter came to his table, took his glass, refilled it, and brought it back. Nader pushed his chair back and I hid my face behind my book as he walked past me towards the washroom.

I got up and scurried to his table, took a glance at two waiters who were busy chatting, and sat down. If he returned and saw me, I could remind him I was Vahid's cousin and had come over for a chat, to tell him how much I admired his poetry. Unfortunately, I didn't have his collection with me, but could he sign the book I had with me? What was my favourite poem? "The old sculptor".

I opened *Rebellion,* "For my dear Nader, Your Forugh", she'd written in pen on the first page. A gust of jealousy twitched my stomach and I had this sudden hatred towards Nader akin only to what I'd felt for Nasser a few years back. I'd seen his friends teasing him for being a germaphobe. I picked up his glass, and while taking a sip, spun it in my hand over my lips to make sure my saliva was all over the edge. I took *Rebellion* and left.

I threw the book in the first rubbish bin I passed by after looking at her handwriting one last time. I was a practicing Muslim. And I'd just stolen from, and basically fed my saliva to, another Muslim. *He's not a Muslim! I bet he even looks down on all the Muslims. He's a playboy who takes advantage of vulnerable women!*

After that, I controlled the urge to visit the café for another three weeks, until I left Tehran for Kermanshah where I'd been stationed for my military service.

*

Over the two years of my military service, I didn't see Forugh. Not that she left me. She was by my side all the way through and helped me to cope with the physical and mental challenges of my service. I followed her work closely. *Arash,* one of the newly established literary journals, usually had a poem or two of hers, sometimes an interview. I realised that because of some of her newly published poems, critics had started taking her more seriously. Deep inside, I did not like that.

I also heard about her from Vahid. He continued living in our house, and didn't care if talking about Forugh made me uncomfortable.

"This Forugh of yours, damn! She's crazy," Vahid said the first time I came back home on leave. He was at this party, and she was drinking vodka like water, contradicting everyone and everything. Suddenly she ambled to the other corner of the living room where Mostafa (one of Vahid's friends) was smoking opium. Everybody fell silent, curious as to what she was doing, towering over his head like that. She started telling Mostafa how insignificant a poet, and how pathetic a person, he was. She didn't stop until she'd ruined the party. "Apparently, she does shit like that all the time!"

"I have just finished my three-month training," I responded without hiding my agitation. "That involved waking up at 4:30am to do military drills and hard, I mean *hard* combat training. I have two days of rest before being dispatched to a checkpoint near Iran-Iraq border crossing to spend most of my time standing under the sun." I ran my hand over my shaved head. "I don't mean to be rude, but I cannot care much about this bourgeois affair." I'd heard the word bourgeois for the first time in a Thursday gathering. I was surprised by my boldness and so was Vahid.

"Okay," he nodded. "Fair enough."

You thought this would've stopped him. But it did not.

"Forugh's got a job at the *Ferdowsi* magazine," Vahid said the second time I was back. Her friend, the editor of the poetry section, had recommended her for the position. "And do you know what she did to her?"

"How can I know?" I said in an apathetic tone.

Forugh had gone behind her friend's back and told the chief editor that she could do a better job and should be in charge of the poetry section. "Can you believe that? Now I know why I could never bring myself to like her."

Forugh had started working as a secretary at Golestan Film Studio, Vahid informed me one year into my military service. "Ibrahim Golestan, the owner of the studio, is quite a character. Apparently during the first meeting, Ibrahim told her, 'I know you consider yourself a poet, but I've hired a secretary not an artist. You're here to do your work and to do it well. Write poetry in your own time.' I've never met this guy, but I think I'd like him. By the way, how much more is left of your service?"

Why are you still living in our house? Don't you realise that you've overstayed your welcome, I thought every time I saw him.

*

After the two years of my military service, I started working at my father's shop. He asked me if I had any plans to further my study and I said that I wasn't ready yet. I found the mind-numbing routine of working in the shop liberating. It kept my mind too busy to wander, and my body tired so I slept peacefully at night. I craved the smell of the shop, a collection of interwoven scents that cooled my nerves: saffron, tea, dried limes, dates, cumin, rice, turmeric, pomegranate paste, dried vegetables, and above all rosewater. After so many years, the smell of the rosewater that my father wore as a perfume had found its way into the warp and woof of the shop, to its very fabric. It smelt like life at its simplest, with no complications, high expectations, or crushing anticipation.

I hadn't seen Forugh for more than two years, and I'd managed to ignore the urge to visit the Golestan Studio that hit me every morning. I'd also stopped buying the literary magazines that usually published her work. Maybe the military service had made a man out of me after all, I thought. I intended to keep up the rhythm of my mundane life, until I was free of her.

A few weeks into my return, I noticed Vahid's strange behaviour. He would disappear for a while and then I would see him coming back, mussed up and drunk, crawling to his unit as quietly as possible. I knew he was drinking sometimes, but he never came home drunk out of respect for my father.

One early morning, when I was getting ready to go to the mosque, I saw Vahid stumbling through the yard, struggling to find his key, and then to put it into the keyhole. I hadn't seen him for almost a week—the longest he'd disappeared for. I knocked at his door. He didn't reply. I knocked again. Nothing.

"Coming in," I said, and entered. The whole room reeked of alcohol. He was right in the middle of the room, in a prostrate position, his forehead on a *mohr*. Was he praying? He was drunk and he wasn't even facing the *qiblah*!

I murmured his name. He didn't move. Was he asleep? "Vahid," I said, this time a bit louder. Finally, I shouted his name. He flicked his head and looked at me as his eyes came into focus. He dragged himself towards the wall and leaned against it with the upper half of his torso.

"Are you alright? Do you want some water?"

He shook his head.

"Tea?"

I took his silence as a yes. "I'll bring it in a minute."

"I lied."

"What?"

"I lied about my study," Vahid said. He hadn't become a doctor because it'd turned out to be too challenging. The damn language! He'd learnt French for a year, but that wasn't nearly enough. He couldn't cope with the stress. All those stupid words! He thought it almost impossible to become a physician using a foreign language. He chose social sciences because, like a fool, he'd thought that would be easier. "Everything I said ... that because of its importance and its essential role in blah blah blah, was bullshit," he sniggered. He was barely surviving doing the new major, but when he was rejected, he got so depressed that he couldn't get out of bed. He quit. "I'm a quitter with a big mouth." For more than a year, he was doing almost nothing, reading a book occasionally, spending his father's money. "When I returned, those books helped me talk like I knew shit. Repeating stuff like a parrot, throwing a French word here and there. I'm so full of shit, you can't even imagine."

"You must've really loved her," I said. He kept quiet. "Do you still have her contacts?"

"Whose contacts?"

"The French girl."

"The French girl? I just asked her out to get over someone else."

"Who?"

"Forugh," he whispered.

"Forugh?"

He'd met her at a party while in Europe. "Based on what I've seen I might be the only loser she has ever rejected!" He snorted. It was followed with almost silent weeping. It made me uncomfortable. I left.

I skipped mosque, did my prayer at home, then lay back in bed thinking about Vahid. Now I knew why he didn't get a proper job when he looked more than qualified, and continued writing articles for random journals for almost nothing; why he hadn't moved out yet and wore the same old suits and long coats—elegant as they were—as when he'd moved into our house. I fell asleep with a picture of Vahid in my mind kissing a woman with red cheeks.

Later that morning, when I was leaving for work, I paused at his door to check on him. But I changed my mind and walked away.


When I returned home in the evening I found a note on my desk reading, I have to leave. I'm sorry. I rushed to the living room. "Did you know

Vahid's left?"

My parents looked at me in disbelief.

"What?"

"He wouldn't leave without saying goodbye."

"He left a note," I said.

My mother, who had been long irritated by Vahid for prolonging his stay, took the note and read it out loud. "After all you did for him he didn't bother to say a proper thank you or goodbye. Some cousin you have!"

My father did not say anything.

*

No one talked about it aloud. How did I find out? Intangible whispers. Averted gazes. Angry but quiet quarrels. My father's hair growing white on his temples; hearing him cry after his morning prayers. My mother fidgeting around, cursing under her breath, eating nonstop, putting on weight faster than a pregnant woman would. Zari not talking anymore, not leaving the house, not smiling, not existing, morphing into a ghost. Her face growing thinner, looking old and weary, as her hands and feet became plumper and her floral house dresses grew larger and looser. And finally their silences that were turning into a discourse more informative than any speech. Zari was pregnant. Now we knew why Vahid was sorry.

*

From the day Zari's pregnancy was certain until her delivery, she was almost invisible. When family members were around, she seldom left her room. From my bedroom, I could hear her dress rustling at night. When she hadn't yet grown too big, she would go out with my mother occasionally. If she suddenly disappeared from the public eye, her empty place would be filled in with rumours.

Once I saw my mother and Zari talking to a neighbour in front of our house. Zari was maintaining a forced smile and my mother a broad one, asking her to come in for a tea. As soon as she turned away, affability disappeared and gloom took over both faces once again. We all had one unspoken mission: to keep disgrace within the walls.

Zohre didn't know how to share the scandalous news with her husband, Javad. She couldn't let him lose respect for her and her family, and acted as if she hoped to conceal the truth forever. She'd even planned a six-week pilgrimage to Karbala for the time when Zari's belly would prove too big to conceal.

When Zohre and Javad came for Friday dinners, everybody was expected to behave normally. Zohre acted all cheerful, with her fake smiles, fake words, fake presence. My mother chatted to Javad, fed him to the verge of exploding, and looked for words to break any silence that sounded too revealing. Zari avoided eye contact with everyone except Javad, who apparently had no talent for reading the room. My father, who couldn't even bring himself to look at Zari (more from shame than anything else), conversed with him gracefully. I sat there full of pity for my family, who had to participate in this circus of infamy, and fantasised about beating the crap out of the biggest son of a bitch I'd ever met.

The day Zari was due and we were waiting for a midwife to do the delivery at home, my mother came to the living room and whispered something into my father's ear.

"Forget the midwife. We'll take her to the hospital," my father said, rising from his chair.

"Let me get her ready," my mother replied. But Zari wouldn't leave the house. She was alright and was going to deliver at home.

"Let me talk to her," my father said.

"Wait," my mother replied. She came back after a moment. "She doesn't want to talk to anyone."

*

Zari died during childbirth two months after her twenty-ninth birthday. It seemed like a miracle that such a demoralised body could give birth to such a healthy baby—as if she'd passed all the life that she'd given up on onto him. My mother lost almost all the weight she'd gained, as if she was melting away. My father grew old like a character in a film skipping twenty years. Unable to cry, I was constantly enraged. One day, struggling to open the door, I punched it so hard that I broke a finger. Even the excruciating pain failed to make me cry. Only at night, lying in bed, my stiff body going lax with the painkillers dissolving in my blood would I heave with silent sobs, looking at my middle finger sticking out in its white cast.

When Zohre came back from her pilgrimage, Zari had already been dead for a week. Javad bought the story of meningitis and sobbed like a child over her grave while praying for the blessing of her soul. Her tombstone read: *The eternal sanctuary of the reverend maiden, Miss Zahra Golzar.*

My mother called the baby boy Ali and raised him like her own, as the official story went. What are the odds that you would lose a child at the same time as you give birth to one? I am sure there were people who figured the odds out, but to our knowledge, it never went public—and that was enough.

*

"It's time to go home," my father said, the words barely making it out of his mouth.

"Just wait," I said. I needed to digest what I had heard. All these years, my uncle Ali had been my cousin! How could they hide the truth from him?

When my grandma died, after her burial, Ali and I had walked to Zari's grave nearby. I knew that Ali had this strange affinity with the sister he'd never met, save for her pictures, and occasionally paid her grave a visit. The sister after whose death, his mother was so heartbroken, that doctors recommended another pregnancy to overcome the grief and that was how Ali was born. This was how the story had been passed to Ali and my generation who didn't know the exact date of her death.

Sometimes he felt guilty that he was born only because she was dead, Ali had said, splashing water on the tombstone, wiping water and dust off with his hand, and placing a red rose on it. His mother gave birth to him when she was forty-seven; maybe that was why he was a bit crazy and couldn't read properly, Ali had said with a snort, which had turned into a silent cry. He'd just buried his mother, after all.

My cousin, Ali—a man who had lost two mothers.

My grandpa was gone, my Aunt Zohre was ill and dying, and it meant that after my father I would be the only one who knew the truth. Why did he tell me this? Had he just passed the responsibility of telling Ali the bitter truth or letting him live the less bitter lie on to me? Ali, a man with dysgraphia, who had worked thirty-five years as a cab driver to buy a house and send his two daughters—who he was so proud of—abroad to study. How would knowing this change his life?

"Did you ever see Vahid again?" I asked in a whisper.

"After Zari's death we acted like he'd never existed. I heard my mother cursing him under her breath when we paid Zari's grave a visit for her fortieth-day memorial—and even then she didn't mention his name. We wouldn't attend any party or gathering where his name could come up. I assumed he'd left Tehran. I saw him once in Mashhad after almost thirty years, in one of the bazaars near Imam Reza Holy Shrine."

"Did he notice you?"

"Not at first," my father said. He got on his feet and looked at me with brooding eyes.

"Was he alone?" I asked, staying seated.

"He was with a middle-aged woman, I guess his wife, and two girls in their early twenties, probably his daughters, all three of them wearing black chadors. He was almost bald, with white hair over his temples, thin stubble, a bulging stomach, and stooping shoulders. He wore a pair of brown glasses, their thick lenses accentuated the black patches under his eyes. Not much was left of the handsome fellow he once was."

"Had they come for pilgrimage? Or were they living in Mashhad?"

"I don't know."

"What did you do?"

"I never knew hatred could survive for so long. But it was there, fresh. Maybe because he'd scarred my soul and decades are like days in the soul's reference of time. I thought of calling his name and waiting for him to turn to slap him so hard he would lose balance, and of then turning to his daughters and saying, would you like to meet your half-brother?"

"Do you regret it? I mean, not doing anything."

For a fraction of a second something dark illuminated his eyes and it scared me.

"I was about to walk off, but I changed my mind. I turned back, overtook them, turned into a small alley and waited right at the junction until his reflection appeared in the display window of the shop opposite. I counted to three and took a step into the street and stumbled right into his left shoulder, stepping on his left foot. As hard as I could. The brown leather of his shoe crumpled under my weight, the box in his hands hit the ground and the sound of shattering glass rang through my head. He turned, his face tinted with anger. I looked right into his eyes. His scarlet face turned pale, it was the look of a man who had lost everything in a second—a moment that kept on stretching as time slowed down. Unintelligible words came out of his wife and daughters' mouths, forming a buzz around us. I gazed into his frightened soul, let the hatred settle in, then walked off. I stopped and looked back. He was squatting on the ground, his lower back leaning against the wall, his hands hanging over his thighs, his neck tilted forward. One of the daughters was massaging his shoulders, the wife and the other daughter towered over him, gesticulating in my direction, their angry words reached me in a whisper."

His lips had turned pale. "Are you alright?" I asked.

He sat back next to me, and buried his face in his large wrinkled hands. "My poor sister," he murmured.

# Chapter Five

I woke up with a hangover and a dry pungent mouth. I sat at the edge of the sofa, rubbing my stiff jaw. Had I started grinding my teeth again? Last night, after my father went to bed, I drank vodka soda and passed out listening to Cohen's 'In My Secret Life'. I rushed to the toilet in the middle of the night, dragging my mobile on the ground before the headset was yanked out of my ears, to throw up. While hugging the toilet bowl, as my stomach unclenched, I decided enough was enough. I didn't want to hear anymore. I didn't care that he'd come all this way to share, to unburden, to confess, or whatever it was he thought he was doing. Not knowing was as much my right as knowing. But in the morning, two aspirins, four glasses of water, and a long shower later, I changed my mind. It cannot get any worse, I thought naively.

I texted my students and canceled my sessions for the rest of the week. Then I texted Ellie: "Do you remember you once said that my life had turned me into a drama-junkie? So when there's none, I'll find a way to create it?"

"Yeah, but I think you've improved a lot, babe. Why? You alright?"

"Yeah. I just remembered it for some reason," I texted back.

She called me and I didn't pick up. If she heard my voice she would tell something was wrong. She sent a few more texts to check if everything was alright. Please let me be? I thought. "You always said that I needed to learn to forgive myself and others, otherwise the bitterness would eat me up inside and turn me into a sad shallow man. Easy to say since you don't live my life, a life that never fails to deliver," I took a deep breath and deleted the text. "With my father, call you back soon babe," I texted instead.

I did some chores while he finished his breakfast, occasionally glancing at a book left open on the table next to his plate. Then he sat outside seeming to read, but when I walked to the balcony to collect the clothes that had been hanging to dry, I noticed he hadn't turned a page since breakfast.

He had four more days in Adelaide. When I'd asked him about his short stay over the phone, he'd said that he couldn't leave my mother alone for too long, but now I suspected this wasn't the whole truth. He intended to leave right after finishing his story. The story I did not want to hear—but *wanted* to hear. I couldn't stand another minute inside the apartment, so suggested we visit Henley Beach. "You'd like it, it's less busy, less commercialised than Glenelg." He nodded and got to his feet to get ready.

I spread a towel on the beach and we sat facing the sea, ate peanut butter sandwiches and listened to the nonstop surging and breaking of the waves. We both seemed to enjoy the beach; with the thrumming ocean there was no need for words to fill in the silence.

"Shall we?" he said eventually. We walked to a sunny green patch nearby and he continued his story.

*

Two years of military service, which was supposed to make a man out of me, and one year of indignation, pain, and grief, and yet I hadn't forgotten her. A few months after Zari's death, I went to Golestan Studio to look for a job, knowing what I was really looking for. She was behind the reception desk, talking to the phone and jotting something down on a piece of paper. She had pixie hair by then, and the thin face I remembered from the night in Café Naderi had grown fuller.

I left before she could see me, walked to a nearby park, and loitered in the spring sun smoking a cigarette. Nothing gives a bad first impression like foul breath. I ambled to a convenience store and bought a pack of gum. Leaving the shop, I glanced at my reflection in the window. I could use a shave and a haircut, but when I reached the barbershop I thought, it's now or never, strode back to the studio and asked to see Mr. Golestan before my nerves could get the best of me.

"You have an appointment?" Forugh asked.

Can't you remember me at all? I had three face-to-face encounters with you as a teenager. Is it my bushy beard? Or am I just too bland? Or maybe because the first time was after your nervous breakdown; the second time you were drunk; and Café Naderi was more than three years ago when you paid me no heed with all the heated arguments and loud men. Whatever the reason, why not a fresh start when it's possible?

"No, but I need to see him now," I said after a pause.

"What's your name?"

"Ismael."

Perhaps it was my nervous gestures and trembling voice that convinced Forugh to leave her desk straightaway to fetch Ibrahim.

"What do you want?" Ibrahim asked.

"I was wondering if I could get a job here."

"What kind of a job?"

"Anything."

"You have to try your luck somewhere else, young man."

"I want to work here."

"Why here? Are you one of those people who dream of becoming an artist? Or are deluded that they are gifted?"

"I just need a job."

"Do you write poetry?"

"Sometimes. But I'm bad at it."

A half-smile appeared on his face. They had a driver, but Ibrahim reckoned I could fill in for him sometimes since he had not been feeling too well recently. "Do you mind cleaning the office too, bringing tea, sorting mail, chores like that?"

I did not. I was asked to bring my birth certificate and driver's license tomorrow so Forugh could arrange the rest. I could start for three days a week at first.

"You said it was important. Are you going to lie like this all the time?" Forugh asked.

"It was important for me to get a job," I managed to mutter.

64

Ibrahim chuckled. "And who knows? Maybe you're a better poet than you think."

Forugh turned her back on me and said something in a hushed tone.

"He's going to do some basic chores. I'm sure he can manage," Ibrahim answered without lowering his voice. He didn't like to have his authority questioned about something so trivial.

I walked away.


The rumours about their love affair weren't out yet, but when I saw Forugh and Ibrahim side by side, I knew straight away that they were more than colleagues. I was no competition for Ibrahim (or Shahi as Forugh called him). I knew it as soon as I saw him. He was good-looking, charismatic, a well-known writer and filmmaker, and one of the few who managed to make a living out of their art at the time when most artists were struggling to cover basics. He was also around twelve years older than Forugh, and her previous relationships showed a pattern in favour of older men. He was married with children, however, which could make him vulnerable. I'm going to sabotage this. I don't know how, but I'll find a way, I thought when I left Golestan Studio for the first time.

*

Forugh must have felt manipulated after our first encounter and we had a rough start as colleagues. But it didn't take long before she grew fond of me as a naive young man, nothing like the overconfident men or players she'd been dealing with her entire life. Moreover, I never participated in office gossip, or made any sleazy or sarcastic comments about her outfits or actions, and she never felt my gaze on her body.

As I got used to her presence, the tension started to dissolve and a sense of intimacy slowly grew between us, mainly through the silences we shared when I drove her around in the studio car. One afternoon, I drove her from studio to a pharmacy and then to her parents' house. I was leaning against the driver door, smoking a cigarette when she returned. "Everything alright?" I asked. She smiled and nodded. That was the turning point in our relationship, the moment I became more than a colleague to her and she was ready to trust me as a friend.

A week or so after I heard her citing 'Green Delusion', the first poem she ever read to me. Not just to me, though. It was I and an old woman who lay dying on a hospital bed. Khanum Kuchik was her mother's half-sister, who had spent almost her entire life in the house of Farrokhzads, doing chores like a maid. "And now she's dying alone," Forugh said to Ibrahim. "I need to go to the hospital."

I was done for the day, but Ibrahim asked whether I could accompany her, so she didn't have to drive while distracted and emotional. On the way to the hospital we stopped at Forugh's parental house to pick up a photo album. She thought going through pictures could be good for Khanum Kuchik's morale. She passed me one of the pictures as we were walking towards the hospital entrance. Khanum Kuchik had a stern face, dark skin, small slanted eyes, and a big eagle nose. She was wearing an old army jacket, which despite being oversized couldn't fully conceal her humpy back. Forugh was looking up at her with a smile, and Khanum Kuchik's head was turning from Forugh towards the camera, a second before she looked right into its lens. They were standing under a garden arch, shaded by a grapevine heavy with clusters of fruit. In front of them, was a *hoz* in shape of an irregular octagon with two longer sides which held a shallow pool of water.

"She always wore my father's discarded army coats. Because of her hump, kids always made fun of her on the street."

"Kids can be cruel," I said. I didn't mention that I was one of them.

"She was a great storyteller. You should've listened to her citing stories from *Shahnameh*. No matter how tired she was, she'd never say no to me when I asked for a story."

Khanum Kuchik was lying on the bed under a white sheet, unconscious; only her face, her grey hair spread over the white pillow, and her left hand and withered elbow were visible. Her body looked like a fruit with its juice

66

sucked out. Now that life was finally leaving her alone, everything about her—every joint, muscle and wrinkle—was relaxed, at peace with her imminent death. Even in its most peaceful form, looking at death made me uncomfortable.

"I'll be back," I said.

I ambled along a green path near the hospital, paused to light a cigarette, took a drag as if inhaling life, and stared at my robust left hand, clouded by swirling smoke. In fifty years, it will be wilted and its bones will be frazzled layers of porous minerals, I thought. Does it matter what it holds? What it touches? What it does in between? Should it create, or lust, or destroy, or just learn to be with no ambition, no desire? If death is the end, if you believe that death is the end, then it seems that you can reason for or against anything and everything. A reasoning purely informed by flesh: every mark, every line, every cell, every function, every disfunction, every memory of an interaction with the outside world… A proposition too arbitrary, too chaotic!

When I re-entered the room Forugh was holding Khanum Kuchik's hand and narrating the famous story of the legendary Rostam and his son, Sohrab, at the point where they were facing each other on the battlefield, ignorant of the cruel fate that awaited them. Young and naive Sohrab had just dominated Rostam, who was attempting to trick his way out of his predicament by telling Sohrab that a man with real valour had to prevail over his opponent three times before he had the right to shed his blood. I waited there in silence and let Rostam fatally wound Sohrab, discover his real identity from his wristband and try to save his son's life to no avail for the millionth time. How does it feel to be stuck in such a tragic story forever? I thought.

"You're back!" Forugh said as she turned to me. "This was her favourite story."

"I got you a sandwich in case you're staying overnight."

"That's kind of you, Ismael," Forugh took a small notebook out of her bag and opened it. "When I was a teenager, Khanum Kuchik enjoyed it when I read my poetry to her. It must've been the feeling of being part of the family, more than anything else," she sighed. "This isn't complete yet."

She addressed Khanum Kuchik as if she was conscious and present. "But I think you'll like it. You never liked a story with a happy ending."

*The whole day, I was crying in the mirror*
*Spring had passed my window*
*to the trees' green delusion.*
*My body wouldn't fit into my cocoon of loneliness*
*and the odour of my paper crown*
*had polluted the air of that sunless realm*
*I couldn't, I just couldn't anymore…*
*The whole day my gaze*
*was staring into my life's eyes*
*into those anxious frightened eyes*
*who were evading my fixed gaze*
*and like liars,*
*were taking asylum in the safe reclusion of eyelids.*
*Which summit, which peak?*
*Aren't all these winding roads*
*ceasing to exist in that cold sucking mouth?*
*What did you give me,*
*o you words, you deceivers of the credulous,*
*o you the abstinence of flesh and desires?*
*If I put a flower in my hair,*
*wouldn't that be more enticing than*
*this fraud, than this paper crown,*
*which has rotted on the top of my head?*
*How the desert's spirit captured me,*
*and the charm of the moon distanced me*
*from the faith of the herd?…*
*Give me asylum, o, simple whole women*
*whose slender fingers, from above the skin,*
*trace the delightful movement of a fetus,*

*and in whose collar the air is always fused*
*with the aroma of fresh milk....*
*I couldn't, I couldn't anymore.*
*I go to the veranda and caress*
*the taut skin of the night.*
*The lights of intimacy are dark,*
*The lights of intimacy are dark.*
*No one will introduce me to the sunlight,*
*no one will take me to the sparrows' banquet.*
*Commit flight to memory,*
*the bird is mortal.*

I left Forugh at the hospital and drove to the house of one of my friends who was a calligrapher. "Could you write something for me?" I asked.

"Right now?"

"Yeah. It's just one line."

"Come on in then. What's the line that can't wait?" He smiled.

"*Commit flight to memory, the bird is mortal.*"

The day after was a Friday and the studio was closed. On Saturday morning Forugh didn't show up at work. "She's gone to a funeral," somebody told me.

*

I was jealous of, and at the same time impressed by, how her poetry had evolved. It wasn't fair to live a decadent life and then write poetry like that. I still couldn't find any word to capture the sense of that "that". I concealed my jealousy, but my admiration showed itself in occasional simple praises expressed in my most reserved tone, and in the moments of astonishment my silence couldn't hide.

*No one thinks about the flowers*
*no one thinks about the fish*

*no one wants to believe*
*that the garden is dying,*
*that the garden's heart has swollen under the sun*
*that the garden's mind is getting empty*
*of green memories ever so slowly,*
*and the garden's emotion is like something abstract*
*that has rotten in the garden's seclusion…*
*My brother calls the garden a graveyard,*
*my brother laughs at the confusion of greenery*
*and counts the fish corpses*
*which are turning into rotten particles*
*under the water's sick skin.*
*My brother is addicted to philosophy,*
*for my brother the garden's healing*
*lies in its destruction.*
*He gets drunk*
*and punches walls and doors*
*and tries to tell that*
*he is extremely agonised and weary and disheartened.*
*He takes his despair*
*like his ID card and calendar and handkerchief and lighter and pen*
*to the street and bazaar.*
*And his despair is so small*
*that every night it disappears*
*in the hustle and bustle of the bar…*

When she finished reading the poem (sitting cross-legged on a chair in the studio kitchen, as she held a notebook in one hand and ashed her cigarette with the other) I had a comment beyond my usual reserve for the first time. "What's wrong with philosophy?"

"Nothing. If it comes out of a genuine mouth. If it's not simply a bunch of empty words. If it's not like some idiot who tries to plant tropical fruits

70

in Europe," she said.

Twelve years after her death, when the Revolution had conquered the streets of a country that had been described as "an island of stability in one of the most troubled areas of the world" a few months earlier by US President, Jimmy Carter, I found myself reciting another segment of the same poem—"I Feel Pity for the Garden".

*The whole day*
*there it comes from behind the door,*
*the sound of smashing*
*and explosion.*
*All our neighbours*
*—rather than flowers—*
*plant machine-guns and bombshells*
*in their gardens.*
*All our neighbours*
*blanket their tiled ponds,*
*which are unwittingly*
*the secret depository of gun-powder.*
*And kids of our neighbourhood*
*have filled their schoolbags*
*with small bombs…*

That was when I finally found the word I was looking for. Like "that" was to write like a prophet. And she wasn't just an oracle who foresaw the future of her society when everybody else failed to do so. She was also a prophet of worldly love.

*I'm not talking about the frail union of two names*
*and lovemaking in the old pages of a registry.*
*I'm talking about my fortunate hair*
*with the burnt anemones of your kisses*

*and amity of our bodies, in gaiety*
*and the gleam of our nakedness*
*like fish scales in water…*

That was the irony of my life. I was enamoured with the prophet of love and obsessed with the philosopher of death.

\*

By the time he stopped, the sun was fading and the cold grass nipped at our bodies. We left our spot for a bench near a palm tree, marked with scattered patches of pale sunlight.

"'I Feel Pity for the Garden,' has always been one of my favourites," I said. "I haven't seen another poem when the personal becomes political so organically."

He nodded and whispered another part of the poem.

*And my sister who was a friend of flowers*
*and every time mother beat her*
*took the innocent complaints of her heart to their simple and kind gathering*
*and sometimes treated the family of fish to cookies and sun,*
*her house is at the other side of the town.*
*She,*
*in the middle of her artificial house*
*with her artificial goldfish*
*and sheltered with her artificial husband's love*
*and under the shade of artificial apple trees*
*sings artificial songs*
*and makes real babies.*
*She,*
*whenever comes to visit us*
*and the fringe of her skirt gets tainted by the garden's poverty,*
*takes a bath of perfume.*

*She,*
*whenever comes to visit us,*
*is pregnant.*

"You still have it, right? I've seen it in your study."

"Have what?"

"The musty wooden frame with the line you recited in it: *Commit flight to memory, the bird is mortal.*" He nodded. "I never imagined there was such a story behind it."

"The bird is mortal, indeed!" he sighs. "You know that everybody dies, but for most of your life it's just a fact that has got nothing to do with you or your actions—not consciously at least. Because knowing something is different from believing it, and you can never *truly* believe your own mortality. Perhaps because you cannot imagine a world without yourself; as soon as you try you're there observing from a corner! But then you reach an age that your body turns into a living proof of your inevitable demise despite the failure of your imagination." He sat on the bench with a groan.

The first poem my father had recited was a mix of two different poems. Had she later decided to publish them separately? Or was that simply how my father remembered it? It seemed like the wrong moment for such a question.

# Chapter Six

Working in the studio broadened my social life. I was invited to parties that weren't like any social gatherings I'd seen before, which I only attended to be near Forugh. Most people at those parties were either liberals or leftist artists and thinkers and I felt uncomfortable being surrounded by people with whom I had no connection either intellectually or politically. Moreover, I found all the drinking and revealing dresses offensive to my beliefs. I usually kept a glass of water with ice in my hand. That stopped people from offering me drinks and spared me from explaining that I didn't drink alcohol, and risking judgmental looks or sarcastic comments.

It was at a party, an engagement perhaps, when I met Ibrahim's family for the first time. Fakhri (his wife), Lili (his daughter), and Kaveh (his son). The party was held in one of those houses with a big garden at the north of Tehran, all demolished now and turned into high-rise buildings. It had a large and high-ceiling *iwan* with six tall columns that centred the entrance. A white balustrade bordered the *iwan*, except for at the middle where two sets of staircases like two sides of a trapezoid, led from the *iwan* to the yard. The facade was coloured in white with four vertical windows, wooden-framed and arched at the top, located at two sides of a wooden door.

Forugh arrived later than I expected. People had been talking about her and Ibrahim for a while now and perhaps she didn't feel comfortable being around his family. I saw her enter the yard from my table near a round *hoz*, with a small fountain in the middle. She stopped at Ibrahim's table and had a brief exchange with him and Fakhri (who responded to her gracefully), walked upstairs, passed past two tables of fruits and pastry on the *iwan*, and entered the house. Through the open door I saw Lili, who was around twenty, leave the living room (where people were dancing to 6/8 beats) the moment Forugh stepped in, and join her parents at their table in the yard.

I ambled around the garden with Siroos, a camera assistant from the studio, and smoked a cigarette. He'd watched *Psycho* recently and couldn't stop talking about the famous shower scene, the music, the jump cuts, the camera moving towards the plughole only to exit the eye. "It's such a strange feeling when you watch a movie, and before it even ends, you already know that you're watching a classic, something that will go on living long after you're gone." He killed his cigarette and smashed it under his shoe.

When I returned to my table, a drunk man with a loose tie and a sweat-stained shirt joined me to catch his breath. "Why are you sitting alone, young man? Go inside and dance!" We chatted for a while. "Have some fun, life is too short." He rose to his feet. "It was as if yesterday, when I had my first kiss in the basement of this house." He winked at me.

Forugh, a glass of red wine in her hand, exited the house with Kaveh, a teenager at the time, on her side. They stood together next to an apple tree shaded white and pink with its blossoms. I could tell from their gestures and cheerful faces that they were having a friendly conversation. Soon after two men joined Forugh and Kaveh. In a minute, the amiable conversation gave place to an intense argument. I left my table to listen.

"I've seen your house," said the older man to Forugh, "you live in a place like that and still call *us* bourgeois?"

"Being bourgeois isn't about what you have or don't have, it's about how you behave and think and—"

The younger man interrupted her by reaching for the label on her new coat, pulling it off and placing it in her palm, saying sarcastically, "Here you go! I removed your bourgeois label! Now you belong to the proletariat."

Forugh, tipsy from alcohol, walked briskly towards the house crying aloud, "Can you believe these idiots? They say they've removed my bourgeois label!" waving the label in her hand. The younger man looked at Kaveh and said, "It must be difficult to be around her, to make small talk and pretend nothing's the matter."

Everyone around them fell silent.

"I don't have to do anything. I am talking to her because I want to," Kaveh said, and walked off.

Almost four decades later—after Kaveh had become a prominent journalist and photographer—I read about his death by landmine near Kifri in Iraq, just a few hours after he'd said to his colleague, "When I'm in situations like these, I feel I am me." It made me think that they must've felt comfortable in each other's presence because Forugh was a restless artist and Kaveh was on his way to becoming one.

I walked towards the young man—who was still talking about the bourgeois and the proletarian in an assertive tone—turned my head to the left and, pretending not to see him, bumped into him and sent his scarlet drink all over his white shirt.

"What the hell!"

"I'm sorry," I said, as insincerely as I could, and walked away.

I could see Forugh through the glass window, standing in a corner of the living room with a group of people, chatting and laughing. I poured my water into the *hoz*, glanced at her one last time, and left.

*

It was another party—held in a huge garden in Darband, not too far from Saadabad Palace—that stopped me from attending parties anymore. Like other parties it could be summed up in a few words: drinks, nibbles, flirting, and heated discussions about art and politics.

I couldn't wait for it to end. Ibrahim was travelling abroad and since Forugh would be drinking, I was going to drive her back. The last time I'd driven her home she'd been cheerful, talked incessantly, and joked about finding me a girlfriend, touching my arm and tapping my thigh. Every time she leaned towards me I breathed in her scent of alcohol, cigarettes, and perfume. It smelt like trust and intimacy and took my breath away. Halfway home, she'd leaned her head back, mumbled something, and closed her eyes. I reached a large roundabout and for the next ten minutes drove round and round.

"We're still here? I fell asleep and even had a dream. It felt so long," she'd said. "It's been less than a minute," I'd answered.

Tonight, she wore a sleeveless white dress tightened at the waist with a black belt, a golden necklace with a blood-red ruby, and black shoes with long square heels and a single strap above her ankle. What would happen if I walked to her—interrupted her conversion with the couple who were listening to her attentively—and told her about my feelings as if it were not a big deal, I thought. I glanced at her one more time and retired to the backyard, sat on a staircase leading up to a small door and took a mystery novel out of my back pocket.

"What are you reading?" I heard a voice. He was standing behind me at the top of the stairs. He was tall, in his mid-thirties, with black eyes. The door behind him was wide open and through it I could see a six-seater table in the middle of a kitchen. He came down the stairs and offered his hand. "Amir Pishdad. In high school, I was in love with Persian and French literature," he said wistfully. He naively thought that—unlike most of his friends—he would avoid politics and stay loyal to literature forever. "But now being a physician and a member of the League of Iranian Socialists in Europe, I have not much time for literature."

"How did you get involved in politics?" I asked.

"I blame it on Maleki and his Loiters Party." He Laughed. "It was in the period before oil nationalisation and the Coup of 1953. In that anti-imperialist atmosphere it was almost impossible to stay neutral. One day I attended a Q&A session with Maleki, accompanying a friend who had just joined the Loiters Party…"

I tuned out. I'd engaged in the conversation not to be rude, otherwise I wanted to read my book and make sure Forugh didn't end up leaving with someone else. He finished his story, his eyes bright with the excitement of remembering the day that changed his life forever. I said it was a pleasure to meet him and went to check on Forugh.

She was standing next to the pool sipping a drink, talking to a man in a black suit. I took a seat at an empty table and thought about possible word choices for one of the verses in my newest poem I was finding particularly troubling. I had a sudden revelation and was writing it down on a piece of tissue when two men approached Forugh from behind, grabbed her arms, lifted her in the air and threw her in the pool. I stood up and took an angry step forward before I stopped. Who was I to interfere? She has closer friends here, I thought. Plus, I was angry at her as much as the men.

Silence against a background of chuckling and muttered disapproval. The man in black kneeled down, offered her a hand and hauled her out—shivering despite the warm summer night. The host of the party, who had run inside as soon as Forugh was pushed into the pool, came back with a white towel in her hand.

"I'm really sorry. Let's go inside and change," she said, as she spread the towel over her shoulders. "Fortunately, we're almost the same size," she continued with a nervous smile.

I threw the crumpled tissue in the pool and left the party. She was sober enough to drive.

\*

The before-sunset sky was dotted with grey clouds. The sea breeze had turned too cold for a summer evening. My father was shivering.

"I didn't expect it to turn so chilly," he said.

"Luckily I did." I reached into my backpack, fished out a beanie and a neck scarf, and passed them to him. "Do you want to go back home?"

"Let's stay a bit longer. Let's take a walk to warm up," he said, as he put them on.

A girl in a blue bikini got out of the water, walked onto the beach impervious to the cold, and wrapped herself in her towel. "Do you think if Ibrahim was around they would've still pushed her into the pool?"

"Perhaps not."

"They wouldn't dare to pull a prank like that on a 'proper' woman? Would they?"

He nodded. We ambled away from the beach.

# Chapter Seven

To my father's disappointment, I ignored his dream of me becoming a doctor and enrolled in the University of Tehran in 1961 to study Persian Literature. He didn't say anything, but I saw it in his eyes. During the first semester, my relationship with other students never went beyond small talk, until I met Amir. I was sitting at a table in the department's café when I heard, "Typical reactionary! Which is expected of a fan of Khalil Maleki." I looked over my shoulder and saw a student with a thick moustache pushing back his chair and walking out of the café accompanied by two comrades. I'd seen this trio before and knew them by face though not by name.

"What are you reading?" the young man at the table behind me said.

"Was he talking to you?" I asked.

"Forget it! What are you reading?"

I'd started reading *The Republic* again for the first time since my return from military service. I showed him the cover of the book. He was studying philosophy and thought of *The Republic* as one of the most influential philosophy books ever written. That day he was reading an English copy of *The Little Prince*.

"Where did you learn your English?" I asked.

"I spent two years in a boarding school in England."

"Really?" he had my attention. "How was it?"

"I had a good time."

"What about the people?"

"They were quite nice."

"Any bad experiences?"

"One of the students hurled some racial slurs at me."

"What did you do?"

"Told him to fuck off."

"Who is Khalil Maleki?" I asked. I couldn't recall when I had heard that name before.

"The founder of the Loiters Party," he said. "The Tudeh Party can't forgive him for the split Maleki caused. They were kids when it happened, but apparently the hatred has passed through the generations. Why don't you join me?" he offered me the seat opposite his. "Let me tell you a story about Maleki."

Amir's father had been a member of the Tudeh Party when Maleki had led the split. Those who stayed loyal to the party didn't even want to hear Maleki's name. However, his father, who also had not approved of the split, had still kept up his friendship with Maleki. Amir's father had Thursday gatherings at his house and even after the split Maleki was one of the regulars.

Only recently had he asked his father about that Thursday night, the one that had stayed with him for years, though as a kid he hadn't understood what had really happened. That night Maleki had been talking about de-Stalinisation—years before Khrushchev denounced the dictatorship of Joseph Stalin. At some point one of the supporters of the Tudeh Party insulted Maleki, to which one of Maleki's friends answered by saying that the Tudeh Party was nothing but the Soviet Union's little bitch. At this point things got out of hand. Everybody was standing, shouting, and scolding. In the midst of this, to complete the chaos, their two border collies had started barking at the top of their lungs. Maleki was the only one who had remained in his chair, head down, his ears and bald head blushing red. He asked people to pull themselves together, but with all the raging men and barking dogs no one heard him. Except for Amir, who had been kneeling near Maleki's chair, trying to calm their dogs. At some point, his mother, had said, "Out! Everybody out!" She didn't really shout, but maybe because it was a woman's voice among angry men's, it was heard.

"Are you really a Marxist?" I asked.

"I think light comes from the left," he smiled. "But I'm not supporting any ideology *per se*. I think you should read this," he waved *The Little Prince* in the air. "I'll bring you the Farsi version."

I shook his hand and another friendship of mine started with that hand-shake.

*

Amir had studied in England and travelled all over Europe with his parents before he was even eighteen. With a mother who had studied theatre in France and worked as a playwright and a father who was a famous composer, his life was alien to me. I found it alluring without being willing to admit it.

Because of his parents' love for philosophy, literature, and art, his family regularly hosted the most famous writers and intellectuals of the time. Amir would regale me with tales of the eccentric people who attended those gatherings.

"Among the artists who frequented our house was this luscious actress in her late twenties and you can't imagine—"

"Who? Is she famous?"

"I'd rather not to tell, but let's call her Mahvash. Man, you should've seen her! When I met her for the first time, I was reading *Gone With The Wind*, and throughout the book I imagined her as Scarlett O'Hara. And it wasn't just her looks, but her hedonistic take on life that made her all the more irresistible—"

"What does hedonistic mean?"

"Pleasure-seeking."

"Why don't you simply say pleasure-seeking then?"

"Just shut up and let me finish my story."

"Maybe I'm not interested in your *stupid* story," I said, but I knew I was.

He had just turned seventeen when his family was invited to a party to celebrate some rich guy's ninetieth. Mahvash was there too. Throughout the night, Amir looked for an opportunity to initiate a conversation. Late into the party, when everybody was drunk and she was surrounded by men, he decided that he didn't have the courage to approach her, and walked away. In a dark corner of the garden, he found a group of teens drinking good old-fashioned *araq*. He joined in and drank *araq* for the first time. Five or six shots into drinking, he returned to the heart of the party and found Mahvash flirting with a man in a white coat who was handsome enough to intimidate anyone, man or woman. However, the drunken Amir was impervious. He approached her, turned his back to the man in white as if he didn't exist, and told her that he wanted to show her something in the garden, something she could not afford to miss. Under normal circumstances he would've overthought the situation, and therefore messed it up. But this time he acted as if he owed her no explanation. She followed him with a smile that read *I know that you just want some alone time with me*. A few steps into the garden she finally said, "What is this *thing* that I cannot miss," with a sarcastic undertone. He turned and tried to kiss her.

"You didn't!"

"I did."

"Did she let you?"

"Nah."

"So, she wasn't all hedonistic after all."

"Yes, she was!" She just took a greater pleasure in keeping him thirsty, in seeing how desperate he was for her. After that night, every time she got a chance she would whisper in his ear, "Have you kissed anyone recently?" chuckling, letting him smell her perfume and feel her breath on his cheek.

"Are you done with your story?"

"Don't look at me like you've heard the most vulgar story in your life. All men know deep inside that whatever they do, all they really want is to be loved and desired by women."

"You're really good at reducing the meaning of life to nothing but your base desires."

"Life has no inherent meaning, my friend, and the only way to give it meaning is by living it fully."

"And how are you planning to do that?"

He answered my question despite my condescending tone. He was going to live his life by experiencing whatever it had to offer and by not expecting too much out of it.

*

Amir wasn't my only close friend during my time in university. I met Hasan again—a few years after his family had moved away from our neighbour-hood—in the department's prayer room. I finished my afternoon prayers, shook hands with the man next to me, wished him a blessing, and smiled. Hasan! He wasn't the teenager I remembered; he had a fuller body, was slightly taller, and looked more mature with his shaggy beard. Only his eyes, shimmering with a kind of shyness and reserve, were the same. There was an immediate connection, which went beyond our old affiliation.

He'd spent two years trying to get into medical school after his military service, but one and a half years into his study his passion for medicine had faded. Nothing could be more rewarding than saving people's life, but what was he doing when even that bitter artificial fragrance of hospitals made him feel depressed. Now he was in his second year of mechanical engineer-ing. I never asked him what he was doing in the Department of Language and Persian Literature that day.

The first time, Hasan, Amir, and I met at a café near the University of Tehran, I realised I couldn't have them under the same roof. A simple comment on the unusually hot spring led to the possibility of a tough year for farm-ers, the feudal system, land reforms, and eventually the White Revolution.

Amir believed that if the land reforms were done properly, it could create relatively independent individuals; without financial independence, he believed, political, intellectual, and even spiritual independence could not exist.

"You're just repeating the words of that old communist Khalil Maleki," Hasan said.

"He's a socialist. Don't you know the difference?"

"This is a *Muslim* country!" Hasan said. He disliked the Shah, who, he believed, was nothing more than a puppet of the West, but what he despised even more were those treacherous God-less Marxists!

"You insult Maleki without bothering to say a word about his ideas," Amir said.

Hasan dismissed him with a wave of a hand. "I'm not going to waste my time discussing ideas of someone who is an agent of the Soviet Union."

"I don't think any Iranian is despised by the Soviet Union more than Maleki is," Amir said with a condescending smile. The enfranchisement of women that Hasan disliked so much was also a necessary change. We couldn't afford to push half of the country's human resources to the margins of society. He wasn't arguing from a humanistic viewpoint, but from a pragmatic and realistic one.

"Are you repeating Maleki's words again?" Hasan said. "And I couldn't help but notice that you check out every woman who enters this café; I'm sure you'd love to 'empower' them! And you know what's really important here. Getting the British imperialists to cheer for you."

"Now he's suddenly a British agent?"

"Who wants another cup of tea?" I tried to interrupt the argument.

"If you're truly independent *they* won't let you work," Hasan said.

"Who are *they*? And what about you? You're not independent?"

"I am! But people like me are a minority."

"Minority or not, there's a Third Force in this country; those who are anti-colonial but don't wish to submit to the Soviet Union either," Amir said.

"Do you know this Maleki of yours had a meeting with the Shah last time to reassure him that he would respect the constitution, which basically means respecting the monarchy?" Hasan said.

"The constitution isn't just about the monarchy. Plus, we should try to gain revolutionary goals through peaceful means."

"Ugh...like *they* will let you! You're either stupid or naive. This nation has only one road to salvation: going back to its Islamic roots."

"I'm studying philosophy, so I'm always fascinated by ideologies. But one should try not to fall in love with them—love is blind, my friend."

Hasan got to his feet to leave. He didn't need any advice from a petty Marxist.

I introduced Hasan to Entezari too. It was nothing like the disastrous meeting with Amir. He became a regular visitor to the mosque, despite living far away. Discussions with Entezari gave a foundation to Hasan's vision of a just Islamic society and deepened his love for it. A love that changed Hasan's life forever, and shaped his death.

*

"You should learn how to play chess," Amir said. "It's the best game ever invented. Let's go to mine, I'll teach you."

It was my first time in his house, a large duplex building facing a garden of fruit trees, neat patches of vegetables, and a swimming pool hidden behind a line of pink rosebushes. His grandmother, wearing a white scarf, was sitting on the balcony smoking *shisha*. Almost invisible behind a cloud of smoke, she greeted me warmly as we walked into the house. Posters of movies covered the walls of his room. *Psycho, Lawrence of Arabia, 12 Angry Men, East of Eden...*

"How many books have you got here?"

"The real library is my father's. He has this collection of rare, old handwritten books; touching them gives you this incredible feeling. But we have to wait for him to unlock the display shelf."

I was browsing his library when his mother entered the room. She was carrying a bowl of fruit, two cups of tea, and a plate of dried dates on a tray. Her black hair was resting on her shoulders, as it was in the framed picture of her on Amir's desk. Unlike in the photo, where she was wearing a black full-skirted dress, she was wearing a long floral skirt. She was younger than I anticipated and unexpectedly beautiful.

"The apricots are fresh from the garden. You should try some."

"Thanks, Mrs. Jahani," I said.

She left.

"Your mum's so young."

"She had me when she was nineteen. You should see this."

He took out a book from the shelf. *Around the World in Eighty Days*, by Jules Verne. Dozens of autographs covered its first page. Poets, philosophers, writers, literary critics, actors, artists. There were more of those at the back of *Beyond Good and Evil*. He'd been collecting autographs since he was thirteen. Any well-known person who had been in their house during the last eight years.

"What do you think of Al-e-Ahmad?" I asked. Forugh's autograph was next to his.

He liked Jalal as a person. As a thinker...

I wasn't listening. My experience of Forugh had made me feel better when I compared my ordinary life to his. Now I knew she'd been in this house and Amir had had the chance to be around her. He got my attention again when he said, "...Jalal thought Forugh's first collections to be nothing but sexual fantasies. My mother had an argument with Jalal, telling him that he'd missed the whole point. One time Jalal brought a copy of *Arash* to show my mother a good poem of Forugh's. He thought that she was finally overcoming her obsession with sex and was about to write 'real' poetry."

"What about Forugh?" I asked.

"I like her poetry, but I've seen her only twice in my life."

"I see her all the time," I boasted and regretted it immediately.

"Who? Forugh?"

"Yeah," I said reluctantly.

"How?"

"I work part-time at Golestan Studio."

"Really? And it never occurred to you to tell me?"

"It never came up."

"You should take me there sometime."

I could imagine that Amir would hit it off with her and talk for hours. "Ibrahim doesn't like it when people bring their friends to the studio," I said.

86

"We can meet outside."

"I'm not that close to her."

"How long have you been working there?"

I was rescued by Mrs. Jahani calling us for dinner.

*

When you dearly believe in an idea, nothing makes you feel worse than seeing it shattered before your eyes. That was why I'd never mentioned anything about my political inclinations and Ayatollah Entezari to Amir; with him around nothing was safe. In his eyes, I was moderately religious with no real interest in politics.

A few days after he'd tried to teach me chess, I saw Amir again at the university café. Arranging a meeting with Forugh was the first thing he mentioned.

"There's something I'd like to know your take on." I changed the subject. Briefly, I explained to him Entezari's take on governance and Islam.

His face turned serious. He contemplated my words for a while. "Okay, this's how I see it. I find the idea quite unorthodox compared to the common understanding of Shia clergy in regards to political power, and you know that I like nothing more than the unorthodox, my friend. But in this version of governance, *faqih* would be on the top, right?"

"Yeah."

"At the same time, this Entezari of yours wants to empower the suppressed against what he calls the tyranny of the Shah?"

"True."

"To include people in governance you need some sort of a democratic system. Would it be correct if I say that what Entezari has envisioned is something like an Islamic Republic?"

"Kind of, maybe," I said. Entezari never used that terminology himself. I made to get up and order another tea. I'd talked to distract him, but now I felt he was reaching a conclusion which could potentially undermine everything I believed in.

"Just sit for a second," he said. "The problem is that rule of the *faqih* sounds like an elitist doctrine, whereas democracy takes its power from common people. How can you bring two contradictory concepts under the same roof?"

I had no convincing answer for that. "Don't you think you're against this idea because you're against religions in general?" was the best I could come up with.

"You know I'm not against religions. Against simple and absolute answers to complicated questions yes, but not against religions *per se*."

The fact that I had nothing to say made me frustrated, but at least I'd distracted him from the idea of meeting Forugh, which he never brought up again. Perhaps he'd guessed why I'd brought that question up in the first place.

*

"Let's talk to your mother and see how she's doing," my father said.

We entered a café. I ordered two pots of jasmine tea before calling my mother. I wondered if she knew anything about my father's past, and about Forugh. I was almost certain that she didn't. I remembered a day when we were sitting around the kitchen table; my father was reading a newspaper, I was having a late lunch, and my mother was at her tablet, the one I'd bought her when she retired after thirty years of teaching mathematics. I'd installed different apps on it to help us keep in touch when I left the country. One of her friends had sent her a file of Forugh reciting her poem "Earthly Verses".

*Then*
*the sun turned cold*
*and blessing left the lands.*
*And greens withered in meadows*
*and fish withered in seas*
*and earth did not accept*
*the dead unto itself anymore...*

*In caves of loneliness*
*futility was born,*
*blood reeked of hashish and opium.*
*Pregnant women*
*gave birth to headless babies*
*and cradles out of shame*
*took asylum in graves.*
*Such a dark and bitter time*
*bread had crushed the*
*amazing power of prophecy.*
*Prophets*
*wretched and hungry*
*left the promised lands*
*and in meadows' stupor*
*lost lambs did not hear*
*the sound of a shepherd anymore.*

"To write poetry like this, you must be very talented," my mother had said. Nothing in her tone indicated that Forugh was to her anything but a poet.

"You're right," I'd nodded without paying attention to my father's reaction. I would have if I'd known what I knew today.

My father passed me the phone. Every time I talked to my mother, not knowing when I was going to see her again, it made me feel down. This time I felt a pressure in my chest, more guilt than sadness. I said goodbye and hung up the phone. I wondered if she was happy, truly happy. If she'd ever been.

"Do you remember that mum had an audio file of Forugh reciting 'Earthly Verses'? She always murmured *and nobody knew that the name of that sad dove which had escaped the hearts, is faith* when she did her chores."

"Yes. She still does sometimes."

"A dark poem."

"Yes. It is. *Swamps of alcohol with their toxic vapours dragged into their depths the stagnant mass of intellectuals.* And very true."

"Swamps," I whispered. "Payam asked me to go to that protest after the presidential election and I didn't. Then he went missing and my life was never the same again."

"I'm sorry."

"You did something at the time that I never forgave you for," I said. He looked at me with traces of disbelief in his eyes. I'd never talked to him so bluntly. "I was talking to Payam's mother, trying to comfort her, when you passed by the phone and I heard you mumble about naive kids getting themselves and the people around them into trouble." It was only a few days after Payam's disappearance, long before we'd started losing hope. Until then he was one of those who got arrested in a protest and after a while called their family to say that they were kept in custody somewhere.

"I thought that their phone might've been tapped—I know I was being paranoid—and then they would take you away for questioning. I'd almost lost you once, my son."

"Do you remember your advice before I left Mashhad for the University of Tehran?"

He nodded. "Eat a lot of vegetables and stay away from politics."

"When I left Mashhad, I took your advice and stayed away from politics," I said. "And how did that work for me? I never told you this before, but the day they raided my dormitory, I wasn't out protesting with other students; I was hiding in my room. When they finally broke into the dorm, I hid inside my closet, like a coward! They still got me, gave me a beating and threw me off the third-floor balcony. I think the guy who pushed me off, did it, because he was somehow disgusted by my cowardice! I swear to God, I saw it in his eyes!"

He raised his head, threw a glance at me, before he averted his gaze. I pushed my chair back, walked to a small bar opposite, ordered a gin and tonic, and gulped it down. "Somebody's thirsty!" the bartender smiled. I nodded and crossed the road back to the café. The first time I'd drunk in front of my father.

"Are you alright?" he asked. "I'm sorry that—"

"It's okay Baba. I don't want to talk about it," I said and took a sip from my cold tea.

"You know you can talk to me about anything."

"No I can't, let's be real," I said, picked up the pot and tilted it over my cup to salvage the last drops of tea. Nothing.

Outside the café, a boy in black swimming trunks took a group of teenagers by surprise squirting water on them with his water gun. The group dispersed, shouting and laughing, trying to return the attack. Some water splashed on the glass wall next to our table. "Sorry!" A teenage girl smiled and dashed to the other side of the street.

I glanced at his drawn face. "I didn't mean it that way," I whispered. "I'll be back." I left for the washroom, splashed some water on my face, massaged my eyes with my palms, and took my time drying my hands. Back at the table, he was sitting with his hands locked in his lap, his gaze lost in the darkness outside. "Payam liked this girl, they got engaged later, and for her birthday, we searched all the bookshops in Englab Square, to find an older copy of *Another Birth*."

"*Another Birth*," he murmured after a long silence. "I remember the day I skimmed through it for the first time as if it was yesterday."

*

*Another Birth* was an instant hit. She'd already read some of the poems to me herself and a few others were previously published in literary magazines, especially in *Arash*, whose editor was willing to delay print of a new issue if he could have a poem of Forugh's. But now that I read them over and over, and contemplated every word, I could see the maturity in her style, subjects, and word choice in comparison to her earlier poems. This made the title *Another Birth* even more relevant. Ibrahim was there. I could see him in the words and verses.

*My lover*
*with that shameless naked body*
*stood on his strong legs*
*like death.*
*Restless curvy lines*
*are tracing his rebellious limbs*
*within his solid silhouette...*
*He is wildly free*
*like a healthy instinct*
*in the depth of an uninhibited island...*
*My lover*
*is a simple man,*
*a simple man whom*
*—in the ominous land of wonders—*
*I've hidden in the shrub of my breasts*
*like the last relic of a wondrous religion.*

When you find something beautiful, it isn't easy to resent it. I still did.

\*

Ibrahim held a party a few weeks after *Another Birth* was published. No one said it aloud, but everybody knew that it was to celebrate Forugh's latest book. But Forugh didn't show up. It was one thing to be around his family and another to be around them in their own house, under the judgmental gaze of spectators. Ibrahim asked me whether I could pick her up and bring her to the party.

Forugh didn't seem keen on the idea. She hesitated as if weighing her options before saying, "Give me a few minutes to get ready."

"You don't have to go if you don't feel like it," I said.

"It's alright," she almost whispered, "if it means so much to them."

And I knew by "them" she meant "him". On the way to Ibrahim's, I took a wrong turn. I didn't want to take her to the man her book was dedicated to—to the man her love for whom was woven into the poems of the collection. I wasn't changing anything, and the day after he would see her again at the studio. Nonetheless, I couldn't refrain from my sad and desperate meddling.

"Aren't you happy with your book?" I asked.

"It's good that it's published," she said. "Now I can move on." She always felt excited about new poems, but soon found them trivial. She published them as she didn't know what else she could do with them.

"They've received good reviews though."

"I've collected those poems over a period of four years," she said. She considered that lazy. She was almost thirty, but she found her poetry immature for her age. Maybe because she'd never had a proper education.

"And you've dedicated them to Ibrahim." Nobody said anything but everyone knew to whom the I. G. referred to. She kept quiet. "He must be really important in your life."

"Yeah," she murmured to my surprise.

I took another wrong turn. "I don't know what's wrong with me tonight."

"It's alright. I'm not that crazy about this party anyway. I don't know why Ibrahim insists on having me there."

"Isn't it obvious?" I asked.

"You're a good guy," she said, after a pause.

No, I'm not. I detest him for loving you and you for letting him, I thought. "Thanks," I said under my breath.

*

A few days after, while driving Forugh to another studio, I could tell from her dark mood that she was on the verge of a depression. During such periods, she stayed at home and didn't do anything or see anyone. Because of her long history of attempting suicide, whenever her demeanour suggested another fit of gloom, Ibrahim and her friends checked on her to make sure that she would emerge from that mental abyss again—energetic, full of life and creativity as she usually did—without any self-harm.

She hadn't uttered a word since we'd left the studio. I remembered another time when Ibrahim was on an interstate trip and she didn't show up at the studio for a few days. One night after work, two of my colleagues decided to check on her and asked me to tag along.

We knocked, waited, and knocked again. Zahra, her maid, should've opened the door. Everybody was getting agitated. "Where the hell *is* she?" Siroos said before banging on the glassed part of the door so hard that it shattered. We were distracted by taking the small fragments of glass out of his hand and didn't notice that Forugh had opened the door. I smelt stale sweat and turned to see her standing behind us. She was wearing a knee-length white house dress, her hair was tangled into a bush, and her eyes were empty. A pen and a notebook in her hand, she stood there for a second, took a glance at Siroos's bleeding hand, and said in a dull voice, "I have bandages, come." Mehdi followed her in and returned with a gauze and a bottle of antiseptic. "He needs stitches, I think. I'll take him to a clinic," Mehdi said. "You go in, we'll come back later." After they drove away, I took a glance inside the dark apartment, closed the door...

"Oh! An ice cream shop," Forugh's voice snapped me out of my daydream.

"Do you want me to stop?"

"Yes, please."

I turned into a side street and parked the car.

"I haven't been into one of these shops for ages," she said after we sat down at a table. "My mother lived in constant fear of germs." They even took their own cutlery with them when eating out. Once they came to an ice-cream shop like this one and her mother took spoons and plates out of a basket and passed them around the table. Her father was losing it, and she hoped with all her heart that he would contain his anger. But when she placed a plate in front of him, he snatched at the tablecloth, pulled it off, and stormed out without saying a word, leaving them with the broken plates and their embarrassment.

"My father's a raging man, but my mother's not easy to live with either. She had this weird habit of giving her kids enemas, even when they were young teens," she said, tittering, before the gloom took over again. Her father was so cross with her mother. "You can't give everyone enemas," he always complained. She was also obsessed by washing and cleaning. "Why don't you wash the fish in the pond too while you're at it," he would say to her whenever she got into a washing frenzy. "I guess, you cannot ask for a healthy mentality living in that confederacy of dunces, can you?"

She looked at me as if I was the one who could reassure her otherwise. I took a spoonful of the ice cream. It had three layers: saffron, pistachio, and vanilla, with crumbled pistachio on the top. A summer breeze carried the smell of kebab from two shops away. I'm hungry, I thought. She rushed towards a rubbish bin in the street and threw up in it.

"Are you alright?" I asked when she returned to the table. Our eyes met for a second, a fraction of a second, and I knew that she was pregnant.

"We should go." She pushed the bowl of melting ice cream away.

In a few months, with her stomach still flat, I started questioning my conclusion until I read her poem "Rose", a year or so later.

*Rose*
*Rose*
*Rose*
*He took me to a rose garden*
*and he attached a rose to my restless hair in the dark,*
*and finally*
*slept with me on a petal of rose.*
*O, crippled doves*
*O, inexperienced infertile trees, O blind windows*
*under my heart and deep into my waist, now*
*a rose is growing.*
*A rose*
*red*
*like a flag*
*in the day of judgment.*

*Ah, I'm pregnant, pregnant, pregnant.*

I haven't eaten ice cream since. In my mind it tastes like an abortion.

*

We were the last two people to leave the café. My father's eyes were glinting red in the dwelling lights of the night. "We should go home now," I said. We'd stayed out way beyond what I'd initially planned. On the tram, he sat opposite me and stared out the window as light and dark interplayed over his face. From the way his lips moved, I could tell that he was reciting a poem.

"Do you still have any of your poems?" I asked.

"I cannot recall when I stopped writing poetry altogether. But I remember when I started losing interest," he said. "It was a party—" he rubbed his forehead and narrowed his eyes "—the trees were shimmering with colourful lights, so it must've been a wedding."

*

My table was near Sahba's: a poet well known for his mischievous, witty poetry. After Forugh had published "Sin", he'd expressed his willingness to be held accountable for Forugh's sins in one of his poems. That night he was the most popular guest at the party. I was making reluctant small talk with those at my table, and was thinking of leaving before the dinner was served when I heard the word "Forugh" amongst the din. I joined the crowd near his table and saw him getting a small notebook out of his pocket.

"This is not complete yet," he said. He was still struggling to find the proper rhymes for some of the verses. But since everybody insisted, he decided to read it anyway. The poem was about Sahba not being willing to bear Forugh's sins anymore because even a bridge would break under their weight, let alone his scrawny shoulders. I am not sure why I did what I did next, when with every burst of laughter, I wanted to punch him in the throat.

"You should change the word 'song' to 'melody', and use 'passionate' as an adjective in the third verse," I said, and regretted it immediately.

"As a matter of fact that's not bad, not bad at all," he said. "It seems that you have some talent for poetry, young man. Do you write anything?"

"No."

"That's a shame. I think you should."

A week or two later, I was having lunch at the kitchen in the studio, sitting on a chair opposite Ibrahim, when Forugh entered and placed *Khandaniha* magazine on the table.

"Have a look at this," she said to Ibrahim, and flicked through the magazine until she reached the page she was after. By the time she'd poured herself a cup of tea Ibrahim had finished reading.

"If Sahba's making fun of you it means you're doing something right," Ibrahim said.

"I know, it's just pathetic," she said, and flipped the magazine to me so I could have a look too.

I scanned through the poem. It was published with the changes I'd suggested.

A few weeks later Forugh read her poem "O Jewel-Laden Land" to me. It told the story of her getting an ID card.

*I triumphed,*
*I registered myself,*
*I adorned myself with a name on an ID card*
*and my existence was acknowledged by a number*
*so, long live 678, from district 5 of Tehran.*
*I'm not worried anymore,*
*motherland's compassionate embrace,*
*pacifier of historical heritage*
*lullaby of civilisation and culture*

*and the rattle, rattle of the rattle of law*
*I'm not worried anymore…*
*It is a blessing to live in the land of*
*poetry and flowers and nightingales*
*especially when the reality of your existence*
*is eventually acknowledged after years.*
*In a place where,*
*with my first official look through the curtain,*
*I see 678 poets who*
*—charlatans, dressed as bizarre-looking beggars—*
*are looking for rhyme and rhythm in garbage…*

It was the beginning of the end of my search for rhyme and rhythm.

# Chapter Eight

It was past 11:00 am, but my father was still in bed. I'd never seen him sleep in so late. I'd been woken in the middle of the night by ghastly noises, disoriented and hazy, before realising where they came from. My father was having a bad dream. I called him, and when he didn't respond, I walked to his bed, grabbed his shoulders and shook him once or twice. "Baba, Baba!" He opened his eyes, not moving, not saying anything, as if he weren't in this world. In the dim street light I could see his cracked, dry lips. I grabbed the glass of water on his bedside table and passed it to him. He turned on his right shoulder, took a sip, then turned onto his left and closed his eyes. Struggling to fall asleep, I heard the rustle of his bed sheet. He couldn't get back to sleep either.

I mixed some cereal and milk and sat back on the sofa. I typed "Forugh" into YouTube and clicked on the video that promised a declamation of her poems. It started with "I Feel Pity for the Garden". This was Payam's favourite. Previously a fan of literature, he'd lost interest in it unless it was open to "political" interpretation.

Literature was doing more than conveying messages, political or otherwise, I always told him. Perhaps, he always answered. However, as someone who lived under a totalitarian regime that was the kind of literature he was interested in.

This was one of the two poems by Forugh that Payam had found *engagé* enough to write a piece about them in a short-lived students' magazine: *Ayande*. I still had a copy that I kept between the pages of Forugh's collection of poetry. "Years before the Revolution, Forugh had realised that *we* were the cause of the Garden's decaying heart and mind, and if we did not revalue our thoughts and actions, a violent future was waiting for us. She sensed the cancer slithering beneath the skin of our society when every-body else fooled with the healthy appearance failed to do so," it read. I went through the stanzas Payam had included in the piece.

*The garden of our yard is lonely.*
*Father says:*
*"My time has passed*
*my time has passed*
*I carried my burden*
*and did my share."*
*And in his room, from dawn to dusk,*
*he either reads Shahnameh*
*or Nasekh-al-tavarikh*
*Father says to mother:*
*"God may damn all the fish and all the birds,*
*when I'm dead*
*what difference does it make if there's*
*a garden*
*or there's not a garden,*
*my retirement salary is enough for me."*
*My mother's entire life*
*is a prayer rug spread*
*at the threshold of the fear of hell*
*My mother checks everything*
*in search of a sin*
*And she thinks that the blasphemy of a plant*
*has polluted the garden…*
*All our neighbours*
*—rather than flowers—*
*plant machine-guns and bombshells*
*in their gardens…*

I wondered if Payam's family had a copy of the short article that carried the name of their son in print. I should email a copy to his mother, I thought. I typed *The House is Black*, and searched for Forugh's documentary. Less than a minute into the film my mobile died.

"Were you watching *The House is Black*?" my father asked, sitting at the edge of the bed, his face grave, as if he'd returned from a bad dream.

\*

I travelled with Forugh to a leprosarium named Babaqi, twenty kilometres north of Tabriz. A trip with the head of the Leprosy Support Association to the leprosarium had convinced Forugh to pursue the idea of making a documentary about lepers. I thought I'd joined the team to do the driving, but as it turned out, a group of five was going to travel with the studio car packed with the production gear, and Forugh and I took the train. I hadn't travelled much, except to Mashhad to where my parents made frequent pilgrimages to the Imam Reza Holy Shrine. Perhaps she wanted to give me the chance to see another part of the country.

In the train, Forugh sat in front of me, lost in a book. I looked out the window at the slums that were multiplying at the periphery of Tehran, growing faster than the kids living in them, when she said, "This is really beautiful, listen: *I praise you because I am fearfully and wonderfully made; your works are wonderful, I know that full well. My frame was not hidden from you when I was made in the secret place, when I was woven together in the depths of the earth.*"

"What is it?"

"Psalm 139, Old Testament. Have a look."

I leafed through a few pages.

"You quoted this part in an introduction to *The Wall*." I read the bits underlined by her under my breath. "*I am the man who has seen affliction by the rod of the Lord's wrath. He has driven me away and made me walk in darkness rather than light... He has made my skin and my flesh grow old and has broken my bones... Even when I call out or cry for help, he shuts out my prayer.*"

"Yes, I did," she said with a smile. "There's something about you that I can trust."

The comment, which was meant as a compliment, ruffled me. I was hurt by her bold presence that always intimidated me into silence, by the love I couldn't express, and now she was talking to me condescendingly.

"Why did you get a divorce?"

I could tell from her face that she hadn't expected me to ask such a personal question. I had another question in mind, a more vicious one, but I wanted to drag her in, get her to open up, and then go for it when she was most vulnerable.

"Well, I've made many mistakes in my life, but the biggest one, I guess, was getting married when I was too young," she said. She couldn't stand living in her father's house anymore, and she couldn't freely be with Parviz outside of marriage. So she told him to ask her father for her hand. Parviz was funny, cultivated, and a true gentleman. She later hurt him with the divorce and some other stuff, which were among her regrets in life.

"What was wrong with your parents' house?" I asked.

"My father!" she said. "He loved his kids, but he never showed us any affection, as if he was afraid that it would undermine his authority. He wanted absolute obedience from us, as if it were an army base not a family house." She found that ridiculous, considering he was such a rebel himself. Sometimes she wondered if he'd ever thought that it was his blood running through their veins. If he wanted unconditional obedience from his children, he should've adopted. That way he would've had a better chance of getting what he was after.

"Isn't one expected to strictly follow orders in the army? How could he be a rebel?"

"He left his family to avoid a levirate marriage. He was only fourteen," she said. He came to Tehran, did odd jobs to survive and finally joined the army. Once she asked him why he had joined the army. To make a living, because life was tough and to survive one needed to be tougher than life, was his answer. When she started writing poetry he was supportive at first, but as soon as he thought it was bringing shame to the family he asked her to stop, as if it had an on- and off-button.

"He likes poetry? That seems strange for the man you are describing."

She looked out the window and sighed. "Tell me about the complexity of the human mind." There were times she eavesdropped on him walking around his room, reciting poetry and crying. He was a hopeless romantic and compensated for that by putting on a tough act.

She ran a quick hand over her right eye. Had she just cleared away a tear?

"I still don't get it. Why did you get divorced? Why did you *choose* to leave your son?"

Her left eye jerked once and then twice; her lips almost disappeared as her mouth tightened; her eyes sparked with spite. I'd never imagined someone so beautiful could turn that ugly. She pulled herself together and said, "You're so naive! We always talk about people making choices. But not everyone has one. If you're restless with lust for something—it can be poetry, art, science, anything—then do you really have a choice? If you feel miserable not devoting your life to that one thing which you think you're born to do, then the choice is already made for you. It's just a matter of time before you give in. I'm not saying we don't have free choice in life. I'm just saying we don't have it for everything. There's something inherently mediocre about having a choice."

We didn't talk much afterwards. She got back to reading and I lay back to silence the throbbing pain behind my eyes.

*

Forugh named the documentary *The House is Black*. We stayed at the leprosarium for twelve days. She spent the first three days building a relationship with the lepers as she ate with them, talked to them, and listened to their stories, concerns, and complaints. At the time, leprosy was regarded as more contagious than it really was. I couldn't understand how she was willing to sit at their *sofreh* and eat with them. She has attempted suicide so many times in her life that death has lost its menace for her, and has no power over her anymore, I thought. But leprosy promised more than just death. Disfigurement. Stigmatisation. Isolation.

I couldn't quell the fear of getting sick, of being consumed by death ever so slowly, and became obsessed with my hygiene. I washed my hands repeatedly, had a shower twice a day, and often came up with some excuse to avoid eating with the team. One afternoon they had tea around a small table in one of the rooms allocated to us by the head of the leprosarium during our stay. I was passing by the door when they put me on the spot by asking me to join in. I couldn't come up with any excuse to refuse. I poured a cup of tea from the samovar at the corner of the room and sat on a chair. At some point Forugh picked up my cup by mistake and as she took it to her lips, I blurted in fright, "That's mine!" Everybody fell silent and looked at me. "I've already taken a sip," I lied.

"It's alright! I don't mind." Forugh put my cup back and picked up hers.

"I crave a cigarette, anybody care to join me?" I asked in a minute. No one. I left, smoked a cigarette, threw the tea away and returned.

My fears found their way into my dreams. In one dream, I was standing behind Forugh, who was squatting next to a boy, talking to him, and playing with tiny stones. I wanted to tell her that I was tired of chasing her around. That I wanted to have nothing to do with her anymore. "You're not worth it," I wanted to say. But what came out of my mouth was cryptic, incomprehensible. Forugh turned, a leprosy lesion on her face, and said, "As long as it's not spread to your soul, it's okay." And I had this sudden realisation that my tongue, nothing more than a stub now, had been consumed by leprosy. I woke soaked in sweat. Of course I never showed her my concern; I had concealed my fear of leprosy just as I'd hidden my desire for her.

When the crew worked, I hung around in case they needed anything. Once Forugh asked me to go shopping for a wedding between two lepers planned for that evening at the asylum. When I returned she was dancing, lepers clapped and took turns to join her in the middle of the circle. I passed her the boxes of cake, pastry, and fruit and walked to my favourite spot, the corner of a far-off staircase that was rarely used. I saw her waving

104

at me, pointing at the piece of cake in her hand, asking me to join in. I shook my head, lit a cigarette, and sat on the stairs.

When we finally left, I was relieved. On the train there were three of us now. A kid was sitting next to Forugh, leaning his face against the window. Forugh had adopted Hosein, asking his parents in the asylum to let her take him to Tehran, promising she would take care of him like her own son. He wouldn't be at risk of getting sick, would have a proper education and a bright future. No parents living in a leprosarium could resist such beautiful promises, no matter how painful the separation.

Forugh slid her body towards Hosein and dragged his stiff body into her embrace. "You and my son are so alike. When you see his picture you'll know what I mean. What's your favourite food? My cooking isn't any good, but my mum's a superb cook. I'll ask her to cook it for you." Hosein nodded his head without saying what his favourite food was.

How are you going to fit him into your busy life? I thought. You know you can't leave this one, don't you?

*

I invited Hasan to the opening night of *The House is Black*. He wanted to know who else would be there. "Amir," I said.

"You know I don't like to be around Mr. Know-It-All!"

"It's just to watch a movie."

"As long as he doesn't try to lecture me."

"He won't. I promise."

The movie theatre was full. The Shah's wife, Farah, and his sister, Ashraf, were among the guests. They were sitting at the first row along with the film crew, the second row behind them was kept empty, and I was at the third row with Hasan and Amir.

"If I knew these bastards would be here I wouldn't have come," Hasan said.

"But you did, so shut up and let us watch," Amir said.

"Can you two behave like adults?" I interfered.

"Look at those two phonies clapping so hard," Hasan said when the movie was finished, pointing at Farah, who was now wiping her tears. "I wish I could throw something at them."

Amir took a candy out of his pocket and put it in Hassan's hand, "Go ahead. It's not going to hurt them and it can carry your sweet message across."

"Are you two crazy?" I grabbed the candy out of Hasan's hand.

The royal family and their companions stood up to leave the theatre. People around them rose to their feet, but Forugh stayed seated. They stopped to speak to her, but she still didn't move. I could see the uncomfortable look on people's faces. Farah conversed with Forugh for a few seconds and shook Ibrahim's hand before departing. As they passed us, Amir looked at Farah and gave her a lively smile, which she returned gracefully, but he stayed seated. Hasan put his hand on my right knee, which helped me to overcome the urge to stand up.

On the way out, Hasan was exhilarated. "Thanks for inviting me! The real show was at the end. Man, that just made my day! Honestly, she's turned out to be quite alright," he said with a smile. "Who feels like tea?"

Amir had to leave. Hassan and I strolled to a traditional café with a *tea and shisha* sign. It was loud, served nothing to drink but strong black tea, and everyone inside smelt of tobacco and hard work.

"Do you remember that one time when I confronted Davud?" Hasan asked. "I couldn't hang out with you guys until his family left the neighbourhood."

"Why didn't you say hi to Forugh today? You were playmates as kids," I said. I would never have asked Amir such a question. It showed how incapable of romance and desire I assumed Hasan to be.

"That was ages ago. She may not even remember me."

"Of course she would."

"Did you know Forugh and I share the same birthday? When I was little her brother, Freidun, was my closest friend and we played in their yard all the time," Hasan said. Forugh always followed them around and they ignored her. One time they were standing at the edge of the balcony peeing into the garden when Forugh, five at the time, appeared behind them. Freidun mocked her, saying she couldn't pee standing up. Of course she could! She stepped forward, took off the pantyhose she was wearing under her dress, and tried to pee into the garden. It hit everywhere but the soil. She didn't stop and instead tried to bend further backward.

Hasan laughed and signalled to one of the busboys, asking for two more teas. "I jumped out of my skin as Mrs. Farrokhzad rushed to the balcony shouting and cursing. You know how obsessed she was with cleanliness. I guess urine was the ultimate untouchable for her." He had dashed for the yard door as Mrs. Farrokhzad clutched Forugh's right arm and smacked her head. He ran back home, but when he heard the sound of water mixed with scolding, he climbed a chair on the balcony and peeked over the wall. Forugh was standing at the same spot, naked, covering her crotch with both hands while her mother held the hose right on top of her head. Forugh raised her head, their glances met, and he ran for his room. When he found the courage to come back, no one was around. Her green dress and white pantyhose were hung out to dry. Her red sandals were propped against the wall, under the sun.

Hasan stared at the cup of tea in front of him. His cheeks were flushed, by childhood's memories or hot tea? I couldn't tell. "I can't approve of her lifestyle, of course, when it's against everything I believe in," Hasan said in a low tone. He'd read that piece, the one that had "Sin" attached to it; he'd heard about the scandals, and was disappointed. "But tonight she reminded me of that little girl who was stubbornly trying to pee standing up."

How did the story make me feel? Mediocre? Inferior? Creativity was not the only thing I couldn't match her in; I could never be as bold, as daring. It showed how different we were, how incompatible. How much of a fool I was, obsessing after a woman I could never have.

"Have you read her latest collection?" he asked. "Are there any of her poems that you particularly like?"

"I don't feel well. I need to go home," I said.

*

Forugh had referred to poets like me as "charlatans" and "bizarre-looking beggars" in her poem "O Jewel-Laden Land". However, it wasn't the only poem whose world of words I found my way into.

She and Ibrahim returned from a short business trip in the green north. Her skin was radiant and her eyes shone with something that could only be happiness. Everyone was already aware of Forugh and Ibrahim's affair. But I thought if the word was officially out, then Ibrahim's wife would have to react, do or say something that could sabotage the affair. The day after, I wrote a piece titled "The Hypocrisy of Pseudo-intellectuals of Our Time", signed it with a pen name, and sent it to *Ferdowsi* magazine. I didn't get my hopes up; however it was published in two weeks.

Now that my words were printed, they seemed to become more convincing, more vicious. In the article, I'd referred to Forugh's wishes for women's progress, those mentioned in the piece that contained "Sin" published in *The Intellectual* a few years back. I talked about how her mother was the victim of a concupiscent husband who had maintained another wife or lover next to his first wife for almost all his married life; how Forugh and her siblings were affected by nerve-racking fights and never-ending quarrels caused by their father's insatiable lust for women. I also mentioned the story of Forugh's father pointing his gun at Forugh's mother after she'd ambushed his second wife and beat her up. (The story became a dark joke that made everybody in our neighbourhood smile nervously.)

Now, Forugh herself was having an affair with a married man. As a so-called intellectual and as someone who had firsthand experience of the demeaning effects of such a relationship on a family, she should've refrained from and condemned such relationships more than anyone else. If starting such a relationship could be justified by our flawed nature, by asking who had never given into temptation of one sort or another, what excuse could one have for continuing it for years? An impulsive act of dishonesty could be pardoned, but not a systematic one. At the end of the day, what could it be called but hypocrisy?

Two days after its publication I saw Forugh at the studio. Her gloomy mood was accentuated by her wrinkled clothes, plain face, and dark patches under her eyes.

"You look..." I couldn't find the right word. "Is it because of the article in *Ferdowsi*?"

"You've read it too? What do you think?"

I said nothing. I had nothing to say.

"I'm not upset for myself. I'm used to this," she said. She felt bad for Shahi who had never seen his wife so down, so miserable. In return, Forugh had never seen Shahi so depressed, so helpless. She fell silent for a while, but I felt the rage that was brewing inside her, as it wrinkled her face and narrowed her eyes, before exploding into words. "I can't believe those bastards out there! Do they think they know me? Or Shahi? Those newspaper worms with their sad little lives are not even man enough to use their real names!"

She left the studio and didn't return for the rest of the week. The day she came back to work, during the lunch break, she asked me if I had a minute.

"I've made a new poem. Do you want to hear it?"

That was how she talked about writing poetry: "I've made a poem." The poem she read to me that day, "Only Sound Remains", is my favourite among her works, even though nothing can make me feel more embarrassed than reading or listening to it.

*Why should I stop, why?*
*The birds have gone in search of the blue direction*
*the horizon is vertical,*
*the horizon is vertical and movement: fountain-like...*
*And day is a vastness*
*which doesn't fit into the limited imagination of*
*newspaper worms.*
*Why should I stop?*
*The path passes through the capillaries of life*
*The cultivating environment of the womb of the moon*

*will kill the corrupt cells*
*and in the chemical atmosphere after sunrise*
*it is only sound,*
*sound that will be absorbed by the particles of time.*
*Why should I stop?...*
*The unmanly one,*
*has hidden his lack of manliness in darkness,*
*and the cockroach ... ah*
*when the cockroach talks.*
*Why should I stop?*
*Collaboration of lead letters is in vain,*
*Collaboration of lead letters will not save the lowly thought...*
*I'm a descendant of the trees*
*breathing the stale air depresses me*
*a bird which had died advised me to commit flight to memory.*
*The ultimate object of all forces is to be united,*
*to be united with the origin of the bright sun,*
*and to be poured into the light's intelligence.*
*It's natural that windmills rot.*
*Why should I stop?*
*I hold the unripe bunches of wheat under my breasts*
*and breastfeed them...*

Had she noticed that my ears were burning red? That I couldn't raise my head, trying to avoid her eyes? I felt beaten like a boxer trapped in a corner. Was she suspicious of me? There was no way!

*What have I got to do*
*with the lengthy howling of wildness*
*in animals' sexual organs?*
*What have I got to do*
*with the pathetic movement of a worm*

*in a fleshy vacuum?*
*The bleeding ancestry of flowers has committed me to life.*
*Do you know the bleeding ancestry of the flowers?*

"It's beautiful," I said with the little breath left in me, and I meant it. Nothing can justify what I did. However, at times I console myself by thinking that if the "unmanly one" and his "lowly thought" hadn't provoked her, maybe one of her most beautiful poems would never have been written.

*

My father fell silent. The wrinkles on his forehead deepened and his thin lips pressed together tightly. He threw a glance at me, wringing his anxious hands. I'd never seen this look in his eyes before. As if now that he'd confessed his act of duplicity to a loved one, now that he couldn't ignore or suppress it anymore, couldn't escape its consequences, it had finally become real.

I couldn't stand his forlorn face, his trembling hands. I got onto my feet to escape the apartment. "Please stay, my son," he pleaded in a tone as if he were afraid that if I left I would never come back. I remembered a scene from my childhood. I was playing at the playground in a park with other kids. My father was sitting quietly in the middle of a bench—not leaving enough space on either side for anyone to sit—as other adults chattered and laughed. Unlike other parents, he never told me it was time we left, rather he let me tire myself until I wanted to go home.

I busied myself with the dishes. I took my time, soaping and rinsing every piece scrupulously. Then I scrubbed the sink spotless, and rearranged the dishes and bowls in the cabinet. When I looked over my shoulder he was still in the same place, same posture, his hands just as restless.

I looked for something to change the subject and the mood. "Did you stay in touch with Ayatollah Entezari while you worked at Golestan?" The muscles in his face loosened up, and his hands relaxed in his lap, but it took him a while before he spoke again.

# Chapter Nine

Grand Ayatollah Borujerdi, the apolitical head of the Madrasah, had died. Nobody anticipated the consequences of his passing for the country: Ayatollah Khomeini, the most formidable critic of the Shah, no longer felt obliged to refrain from politics. At the time, many people hadn't even heard his name, but I'd become familiar with him and his ideas years before he was a national figure.

Khomeini was one of the scholars at Madrasah, where Entezari was a student and later an instructor. Khomeini envisioned a state that was run based on Islamic laws. At a time when most clergy, including the Grand Ayatollah Borujerdi, believed that clerics should refrain from politics, Khomeini believed that politics was at the heart of Islam. Nonetheless, he didn't get involved in politics out of respect for his master Grand Ayatollah Borujerdi.

In the early sixties, Ayatollah Khomeini attacked the Shah in his sermons on grounds such as widespread corruption, violation of the constitution, and the weakening of Islamic beliefs among the people. I turned into his zealous advocate. Through Entezari, Hasan and I got access to copies of his speeches, both written and recorded, and passed them to our friends at the university. We even managed to spread his words among some leftist students who were frustrated with the status quo, and interested in anyone who could challenge it.

The real turmoil came after the referendum on the White Revolution, the reform program implemented by the Shah. Prominent religious and political figures invited people to protest the reforms and the regime on the streets. The protests reached their peak when, on the dawn of June 5, 1963, Ayatollah Khomeini, who had gained fame by then for his blunt criticism of the regime, was arrested. When the news of his arrest spread throughout different cities, my friends and I were among tens of thousands of angry people who took to the streets of Tehran and other major cities.

Hasan and I tried to convince Amir to join us. "You're a pathetic conformist!" Hasan said when, after an hour of argument, Amir's answer was still a firm no. "I bet you're afraid of dying!"

"That's not why I refuse to join the protests, but of course I'm afraid. We are wired to love life. The mere fact that we are here proves it. We know the absurdity of life, but it doesn't affect—"

"Shut up, for God's sake!" Hasan concluded the discussion.

*

Chaos. Blood. Fire. Police stations, banks, and government offices were razed. No place was spared from the people's rage. During the June uprising, which lasted for three days, tens of protestors (some claimed hundreds) were killed. I would've been killed too if I'd been a few centimetres taller.

I was among the angry mob near the University of Tehran, on a main street that led to Enghelab Square, shouting "Death or Khomeini!" The officers of the Imperial Guard, forming a meaty chain that cut the street off from the square, decided to give us the former. I heard a whizzing sound over my head, felt a breeze-like trace on my scalp, and smelt burning hair. A bullet had buzzed through my bush of curly hair. People were dashing past me, bullets were blasting, bodies were hitting the ground, but for a moment I stood there dazed, my ears buzzing, the faint sounds of shrieking, crying, and crashing coming from far away. Hasan clutched at my jumper when he passed me, and it was only then that I turned and started running. Nonstop. Like a crazy person. Only when I was far from the heart of the riot, did I stop and bend over, hands on my knees, gasping for breath. I saw Siroos, standing next to his car, parked in front of a pharmacy, waving at me. I didn't know whether I should trust my vision, blurred with sweat and lack of oxygen, or not. I rushed towards his car and got in.

He popped a pill, swallowed it dry and started the engine. He was talking on and off but I wasn't in the car. I was standing over my corpse, lying on the street, decorated with my blown-up brains, trying to control the shiver that was taking over my body, as the sirens wailed—a fire truck here, an ambulance there. He stopped the car. It appeared that at some point along the way I'd given him my address.

"Thanks for the ride," I said.

"You look pale. Go and get some rest," he said, and looked at my trembling hand for a second before averting his gaze. I put my hand in my pocket. He hunched to get in the car, but then he straightened up his body and said, "Take good care, okay?"

*

I changed the usual route I took to Golestan Studio so as not to pass by the mosque. I wasn't sure why. Something had changed within me, but I still couldn't comprehend it, not fully at least. I hadn't visited the mosque for almost a week when Entezari came to check on me.

"I didn't feel that well the past couple of days. Why don't you come in?" I said. I almost died, I thought.

He only had a few minutes. The regime had kept Ayatollah Khomeini in custody. There were rumours that they were planning to try and execute him. "We can't let that happen," he said gravely.

"What should we do?" I said. I almost died, I thought.

He'd arranged a meeting with some clergy and political activists in his house to discuss all the options and come up with an effective strategy. "You should join us. Hasan will be there too," he said.

"Okay," I said. I almost died, I thought.

He didn't need to remind me that I must not mention the meeting to anyone, no matter how much I trusted them. "You know that SAVAK is everywhere," he said.

"I'll be there," I answered. I knew I wouldn't go. I just wanted to get back to my bed and my book.

"Take care of yourself, my son."

"Thank you," I said. I almost died, I thought.

*

In the weeks that followed my near-death experience, I saw a grey fog surrounding everything and everyone. It eventually found its way into my mind and made me contemplate a world without God, a notion that I found too daunting not to discard fully.

I could've easily died. Like anyone else. I was no exception. I wasn't the centre of the universe. And more importantly, nothing was worth dying for. Or at least, I wasn't ready to die for anything, or any idea, no matter how grand it was. Not yet. Probably not ever. That was a sad realisation.

*

Maybe I should tell her how I feel, I entertained the thought. What was the worst that could happen? After that close-up encounter with death, nothing really mattered anymore. It seemed that I'd lost the ability to take anything seriously, and everything I did felt pointless. At the same time, and strangely enough, the collection of all these trivial, futile affairs formed something called my life which seemed like the one thing that truely mattered, like the only tangible refuge.

One somber autumn night, I decided to walk home after work. On the way, I entered a bar. I wasn't sure why. That night, for the first time in my life, I had a drink. And another one. After a few shots of *araq*, cheap and strong, I was adamant that I would talk to her—tonight. I had one last shot and left the bar. Walking towards her house, the wind didn't feel as cold anymore. The alcohol had penetrated all my layers, soaked my masks and melted them away, even those I wasn't aware of. I could hardly hear the nagging voice in my head, the one that never left me, that spoke for all my doubts, uncertainties, and insecurities. Why I'd never told her the truth? What was the point of all the suffering I'd put myself through so far?

Looking at the dark house, I knew she was out. I felt strangely calm as I pulled my beanie down my forehead, wrapped myself tightly inside my overcoat, sat and leaned against a tree, and closed my eyes. I jolted out of a slumber as her car turned into the driveway. She stepped out of the car and walked straight towards me.

"Ismael! What are you doing here?"

For a second I was sober again and everything felt more complicated than I'd imagined.

"I don't know."

"Have you been drinking?"

"Yes."

"I didn't know you were a drinker."

"Me neither."

She chuckled. She was tipsy too. "It's alright. We need to get some tea into you, into us. Come on in."

We entered the front yard. I was still drunk, but beginning to feel cold again. A shiver was about to overtake me when she opened the door to her living room and a wave of soothing warmth washed over me.

"You don't need to take your shoes off. Just stamp them clean on the mat," she said, as I struggled to get my boots off.

I forced one off. The second one had an impossible knot.

"Come on in now! The house is getting cold."

I gave up on it, went into the living room and closed the door behind me, feeling uncomfortable and embarrassed with only one shoe on. How can I talk to her, looking like this? I thought. "Beautiful house," I said.

"Well, it's Shahi's. I'm just living here. You once came to my old house with the guys, right? That was too cramped. Let's have a warm drink, take some rest, and then I'll drive you home."

"I can't go home."

"Why? Because you have only one shoe on?" she said, laughing. I looked down at my brown muddy boot next to my white, wet sock and smiled.

"My parents can't see me like this."

"It's okay. Sleep here then. And I'll get you scissors for that," she said referring to my boot. "Come on in." I looked down at my boot and hesitated.

"Don't just stay there, come in! It's okay, I'm not my mum."

I walked around the carpet and stopped near the kitchen door. She disappeared into the kitchen and returned with a cup of tea in her hand but no scissors. While grabbing the cup, I touched the back of her hand with my finger and in that moment I opened my mouth to tell her everything. However, what came out was nothing but a short undecipherable noise.

"What's that?"

I shook my head and followed her to the coffee table trying not to limp. She poured some vodka for herself. "I'll get my tea later." She winked at me. I took a sip of tea.

"That's boiling hot!" she said

"I know!"

"You're funny." I didn't think so and pressed my front teeth on my burning tongue. "Tomorrow you'll feel better." It seemed that she was referring to my sense of emptiness rather than my nausea.

I nodded.

"Do you mind sleeping on the sofa? Zahra is sleeping in one of the rooms, and the other one smells of fresh paint."

"Sofa is good."

She left and returned with two blankets. "Tonight's freezing cold."

"Thank you," I said.

"Tomorrow we can go to work together."

She took her half-drunk glass, walked halfway to her room, hesitated, turned, and took the almost empty bottle of vodka.

"Drinking wasn't what I expected it to be," I said.

"Nothing ever is."

"Do you enjoy it?

"I'm not sure. Remember that summer when there was a rumour about an earthquake in Tehran?" she asked. That night she was sleeping with her bird in her car when Shahi came and took her to his place. She slept in the yard, on a bed near Kaveh's. He slept in his room; he believed that nothing would happen. Anyway, he had to sleep next to his wife. The whole night, she listened to crickets singing, her eyes fixed on the window of his room, hoping to see his shadow passing by. "My whole body was aching with the pain of wanting and not being able to. What a painful thought that if the earthquake really had happened we could've died away from each other."

She stood there, staring into the dark corner of the room, bottle in one hand, glass in the other, the liquor swirling softly inside, following the circular movement of her wrist. "Everyone has a soulmate, she should find him, sleep with him and then die."

"How do you know someone is your soulmate?"

"If you experience those rare moments with him, moments of clarity, when you see how absurd yet beautiful life is. I know that I'd be the first one to die in my family." She gulped down her drink. "I don't know why I'm telling you all these," she whispered. "Good night."

She closed her bedroom door without pushing it fully into its frame. Some light poured from the thin crack. In a minute, the light was off and the bedside lamp on.

I must leave! I got to my feet, but lost balance and fell back onto the sofa. I closed my eyes to stop the world from spinning. I woke from a dreamless sleep without any sense of time. It might've been five minutes or a few hours. I rushed to the toilet and threw up. I squeezed some toothpaste onto my finger and washed my gums and tongue to get rid of the foul taste in my mouth.

My left foot throbbed inside the boot. I sat back on the sofa, took a knife from the coffee table's open shelf, cut the lace open, and took the boot off. With my burning foot on the cold soothing floor, I leaned my head back and rested my eyes for a minute. Then I walked to her door, pushed it open and stayed at the entrance. The bathroom light, which I'd forgotten to turn off, travelled through the living room to her room and highlighted her silhouette under the blanket. I raised my right foot and landed it over the threshold in her room. I'd crossed a line, literally and figuratively.

I started walking around her bedroom. I looked inside her closet, ran my fingers over her clothes, and inhaled the remnants of her familiar scent. A touch of the knee-length red-and-white-striped silk dress was enough for my body to forget its mortality, and for my brain to abandon the bit of concern it still reserved for my forbidden presence. I checked her dresser, picked up a lipstick, opened it, rubbed it on the back of my hand, closed it and put it back again. Next to the empty bottle of vodka on her bedside table, resting on a small notebook, I noticed a silver necklace with a square pendant that contained a prayer to keep away the evil eye. She wore it almost all the time: a gift from her grandmother. I picked the notebook up. It was an old calendar similar to the one she'd had with her in the hospital a couple of years back. I leafed through and read pieces of her poems, some new, some old and already published. There was an extended version of the poem she'd read over Khanum Kuchik's bed, the one published in *Another Birth*, titled "Green Delusion". I noticed another long poem with no name yet.

*I said to my mother, "It's all over."*
*I said, "It always happens before you expect it.*
*We have to send condolences to the newspaper's obituary page."*
*Hallow human*
*hallow human full of confidence*
*look how his teeth sing*
*while chewing,*
*and his eyes*
*how they slit*
*while staring.*
*And how he passes by the wet trees:*
*patient,*
*grave,*
*confused…*

A morbid feeling came over me and I put the notebook back. A perfect silence, except for the occasional breeze rustling through the branches outside, and my heartbeat inside. She was sleeping on her left side. I sat next to her bed and listened to her breathing, muted, tranquil and composed. Her breasts, firm and sober even with all the alcohol in their veins, pulsed rhythmically with every breath. Her face was resting on the edge of the bed. I bent forward and half of my lips touched hers, for a second. The smell of vodka and cigarettes. She opened her eyes, and my lips departed. She looked right at me, but as if she were dreaming with open eyes. She closed them again. My body shivered uncontrollably. My brain was back in charge again and I could feel my sex going lifeless. Contracted and wrinkled, as if I'd gone swimming on a winter night.

I cannot remember how I got out. In the yard, I sat on my knees and threw up next to the apple tree. I waited for my stomach to unclench while looking at a wrinkled green apple half-covered in my barf. It cleared my head. I went back inside, folded the blankets and returned them to the room she'd taken them from. I washed my cup, then wiped the floor clean of my shoe prints with a tissue. The empty bottle on her bedside table gave me hope that she wouldn't remember anything in the morning. Perhaps a half-cooked kiss from a man with no clear face in her dreams. I'd left the house and closed the door behind me when I remembered that I hadn't cleaned up my vomit in the garden. Distressed, I bent over and threw up again. I covered it over with soil and dried leaves. I looked at the silver pendant in my hand and put it in my pocket.

I never touched alcohol again.

*

A few weeks after the June uprising, Amir and I met at a café near the University of Tehran. Maleki had returned from Vienna after one and a half years of self-imposed exile. I was going with Amir to meet him for the first time. Before, I wouldn't have been interested, I wouldn't have taken the risk of having my worldview shattered. But now it was already broken into pieces.

I told him how everything had changed. I prayed, but it felt as if my prayers were disappearing into an empty vacuum. I ate, but food did not taste as usual. I had drunk alcohol, something that I thought I would never do even if my life depended on it. I couldn't pass the first page of *An Introduction to Plato*, which I'd waited for so long to find a second hand copy of…

Hasan walked in and sat down at the table. "How have you been? Entezari was asking about you the other day."

"I'll pay him a visit soon."

"Did your mother pass you my messages?"

"Yeah, sorry, but I've been quite busy lately."

"Busy? Busy with what?"

"He just needs some time to himself, God! Read the room!" Amir said to Hasan, before he turned to me. "That's called an existential crisis, my friend. Everybody experiences that at some point of their lives. You'll be alright, I'm sure."

"That's called an existential crisis!" Hasan imitated Amir with the tip of his tongue poking out.

"I stand corrected. Sheep are the exception."

Hasan ignored his comment and took a book out of his bag. "I meant to pass you this. It's a great read."

I skimmed through *West-mania,* by Jalal Al-e-Ahmad. "What's with all the circles?" I asked Hasan.

"I just draw them to unwind." Hasan wondered if it was possible to draw a perfect circle using nothing but his hand. He'd tried different strategies. Drawing slowly, doing it in one fast stroke, drawing with closed eyes, using his left hand. "Some of them are not too bad."

"Yeah. Like this one," I pointed at the near-perfect green circle at the corner of the title page and rose to my feet.

"You're leaving?"

"We've got to go now," Amir interjected.

*

Maleki took his time with every word, like a man who had all the time in the world and nothing surprised him anymore. Soft-spoken, with melancholic eyes, he didn't fit the picture I had of him in my mind after listening to all the stories about him being blunt. In Amir's favourite story, the one he recited all the time, Maleki met the Shah. At some point the Shah told Maleki that he himself was a fan of socialism. "That may be true. But socialism and monarchy don't get along well," Maleki responded. I found myself wanting to witness one of those transitory episodes, when he turned from the gentle man sitting in front of me to one who was uncompromisingly forthright.

"Didn't your doctor advise you not to drink?" Amir asked, pointing to the cup of *araq* in Maleki's hand.

"Doctors! Those European doctors have no idea what we're going through here. If they did, they'd prescribe it instead of medicine." Maleki placed two glasses in front of us.

"He doesn't drink," Amir said.

"What are you doing these days?" Maleki asked me.

"He studies Persian Literature and has a part-time job at Golestan Studio," Amir answered for me.

"Golestan Studio? I know Ibrahim from his time in the Tudeh Party. He eventually came to believe that only art can have any real and lasting influence, and stopped being actively involved in politics. Are you planning on becoming a director or something?"

"I just help out around the place."

"He likes poetry. He's a fan of Forugh," Amir said to my surprise.

"How was Europe?" I changed the subject.

"Quite alright," he said. He had the chance to read and write in peace, and to meet his friends from the League of Iranian Socialists in Europe. When he was here, he couldn't communicate with them freely as SAVAK would read any letters he sent through the post. He always had to find a traveller to pass his letters on for him.

"What's your take on the idea of living somewhere else? I mean permanently," I asked.

"As your favourite poet says: *I'm afraid of the time that has lost its heart. I'm afraid of picturing the futility of all these hands, and imagining the alienation of all these faces. I, like a student who is madly in love with her geometry lesson, am alone. And I think the garden can be taken to a hospital…"* He fell silent, had another shot of *araq*, and then continued with verses from another poem. Was it on purpose, or was it the lapse of a drunk and weary mind? *"…Someone is coming, someone who is with us in his heart, in his breathing, in his voice, someone whose arrival can't be handcuffed and thrown in jail…"*

He stopped. His eyes fixed on the empty glass in his hands. It seemed that he'd lost track of his thoughts. I looked at Amir, hoping he was going to say something to break the lingering silence, but he was playing with the shot of *araq* in his hand, rolling it back and forth between his fingers. I asked the question that had occupied my mind . "Is it a waste of time to pursue politics?" He had another shot of *araq* and I continued with a lower tone, "Do you regret spending your life as a political activist?"

Amir raised his head and glanced at me. I thought I'd crossed a line by asking an inappropriate question, but his face didn't show any feeling.

"Most of my life I worked to further social-democratic ideas," he said. "What we have is not even close, and I can't see it happening in the fore-seeable future. So, yes, I am disappointed. Do I regret it? I've been jailed a couple of times, defamed, even tortured. So, yes, at times. But I got involved in politics to change things for the better and I would go down the same path, if I had a second chance."

*

I visited Maleki one last time before his arrest.

"Give me a minute to wrap this sentence up," he said as Amir and I entered.

"Can you get your works published again?" I asked.

"No." He put his pen down, and got on his feet to pour tea from the samovar, which sat always boiling on a small table near his desk. "Ismael, you asked me a question last time, which I don't think I answered." He placed two cups of tea with a bowl of sugar cubes on the table. "I'm well aware that for a decent man even day-to-day life has turned into a challenge in this country, but I still have hope and I think—"

Someone knocked at the living room door and entered. His head was shaved and he limped as he walked. "Hushang?" Amir said.

"Your son let me in," he said to Maleki. He'd been arrested on the street after leaving the University of Tehran. No one had heard of him for the last ten days.

"God! What have they done to you?" Maleki asked.

"Taught me a lesson," he said with a forced smile.

"Take a seat," I said.

"I can't ... really sit."

"Make yourself comfortable," Maleki said.

Hushang got on his knees and then lay down on his stomach. I saw Maleki's lower lip tremble. He excused himself. Nobody said anything until he returned.

"I'll be alright," Hushang said to Maleki.

"You will be, my son, but not our nation," he said. "By these barbaric responses to peaceful activities, they're pushing people towards violent actions which will eventually write the future of our nation in blood."

Amir offered Hushang a cup of tea, which he got on his knees to drink as he talked about his arrest and interrogation. He was tired, so he left. Without a word Maleki returned to his desk and started writing.

"It's kind of late. We'd better get going too," Amir said.

"Wait for a few minutes, please." We sat back as Maleki continued writing. "Would you mind taking this to the printer's first thing tomorrow?"


Amir stopped under the street lamp outside Maleki's house. I listened to him reading the open letter against the melody of chirping crickets. His face, dimly lit by the yellow lamp, turned fretful as he progressed. It told the story of Hushang (without mentioning his name), invited "them" to learn from history and to think about the consequences of their actions, and finally accused "them" of stealing people's rights to free choice, despoiling the resources of the nation, and ruining its future. Maleki had finished by saying that he was writing the letter so they could arrest him too if they wished to do so. He wasn't welcoming prison, but he was not afraid of it either. He was used to torture, no hair was left on his head to be shaved, and even in his own house, he felt like he was in prison.

"This is going to cause him trouble. Maybe I should delete the last bit."

"You can't do that," I said. He did not respond. "He'll find out after it's published. You know that, right?"

"He can't afford to go to prison in his condition. He's angry now, but he'll understand."

In retrospect, I think that if anything, Amir should've considered taking out the bit where Maleki asked "them" to learn from history. There is nothing a tyrant or a totalitarian system hates more than having history as their teacher. Their very existence is the proof of that.

\*

"Maleki is arrested," Amir said, after I picked up the phone, still disoriented with sleep. "I shouldn't have taken that damn letter to the printer's. I should've waited for a day or two, let him calm down, and talked some sense into him."

"It may not have been the letter. Didn't he meet with a member of the British Labour Party the other day? Anyway, you just did what he asked you to do," I said. I waved at my parents, waiting in the middle of the living room, looking anxious, waiting for bad news, the only kind of news that came after midnight. I reassured them and asked them to go back to bed.

"I hope they'll go easy on him."

"They have nothing solid against him. He'll be fine, I'm sure."

Maleki was tried and sentenced to three years in prison.

\*

I'd heard enough for one night. I took a long shower, hoping by the time I was out my father would already be asleep. Then I could have some alone time. Maybe go for a walk, or have a drink at a bar. His dinner—cheese, bread and walnuts—was still on the table, untouched. He'd taken only a sip of his milk.

"We passed by an Afghan restaurant the other day, maybe we can have dinner there?" he asked. He never cared for dinner, for food in general. He could live on bread and yogurt for weeks without complaining. He was demanding to spend time with his son.

"Let's go another night."

"I'd prefer tonight, if you don't mind."

No matter how his narrative is making me feel, righteousness is not mine, I thought, and got ready to go out. Only later would I realise that my father's insistence on going out for dinner was because he knew what he was going to tell me would change things for the worse.

It was dusk, but the weather was yet to cool. Everything around us, the asphalt, the walls, even the trees, was shedding the heat collected during the day. A few minutes, and he was already struggling in the heat. "Have some water," I said and passed him a bottle. When he was done drinking, two young girls wearing see-through crochet dresses walked past us and he shook his head in disapproval. I was in no mood for an argument, but I said nonetheless, "Women should be free to wear whatever they want to. It's sexist to think—"

"It's what?" he asked.

"Sexist. It means—"

"It doesn't matter what it means. You should know better by now."

"What do you mean? I can't question your opinion?" I said, surprised with the hostility in my voice.

"You can question anything, my son," he said calmly. "Just try to avoid pre-made labels. Ideologies have always used labels to suppress reason and silence any opposing voice."

"I'll ask a question that I think is reasonable then: why are we so afraid of women's bodies?"

"Even if we are, I don't know why. I don't claim to know western culture either. But I'm sure about one thing. They're not afraid of anything that can be capitalised on, that can be commercialised," he said. "At the end of the day none of this really matters," he added with a sigh. "Let's have dinner in peace. Who knows when we'll have the chance for another night out again?"

# Chapter Ten

"Your voice is a bit hoarse, are you falling sick?" My father asked.

"It's the acid reflux, happens every time I eat late."

"I get them too."

"Really?"

"I put two pillows under my head and it helps."

"But the food was good last night." We had Borani Banjan. Eggplants cooked with tomatoes, topped with yogurt-garlic sauce and dried mint, and served with hot naan on the side.

"Yeah, it was. I'd never tried it before."

"With so many Afghan immigrants, I cannot recall even one Afghan restaurant in Mashhad. But why?" He shrugged. I looked out the glass window; near the horizon the city looked like a mirage melting away under the scorching sun. "And you never travelled anywhere."

"No, I didn't," he exhaled. "Forugh was the opposite, though. I'm not sure if she liked it or she just followed her restless soul."

*

In the spring of 1966, Forugh travelled to Italy to attend the Pesaro Film Festival for a screening of *The House is Black*. One day, after sorting out the mail and running a few errands, I sat in the kitchen with a letter in my hand, addressed to Ibrahim. It was the second time in my life that I'd held a letter from Forugh which was written for another man. Stay out of trouble and return it while you can, I thought. Ibrahim was out at the time, and I could take the envelope to his office, put it on his desk, and pretend that I hadn't carried it around in my pocket for the whole morning.

But no. During the lunch break I bought a dozen envelopes and a fountain pen, similar to the one Forugh wrote with. At home, I took a couple of white pieces of paper and jotted a few words on each of them with the new pen. I put each inside of an envelope, wet the flap, and sealed them. Then I boiled some water in the kettle and got into testing my plan. Soon I had a rough idea of how to use steam to open an envelope without leaving steam marks on the envelope or ink stains on the letter. I practiced it a few more times before I tried with Forugh's letter. There it was in my hand, untouched, unmarked.

She was writing from Rome, under the sun and surrounded by sculptures. She'd watched a few movies and had been disappointed in them. Waiting without a goal was nerve-racking and generally she didn't feel well. "I'm constantly facing this question that without you, what's left for me?"

I resisted the urge to crumple the letter in my fist, but I still didn't want to hand it to Ibrahim myself. I followed the line-mark to fold the letter back and threw it into the studio's mailbox the next day. Ibrahim would find it himself at some point.

*

I worked in the studio only three days a week; however, I checked the mailbox every morning before anyone showed up. The second letter came in a week. She felt nauseated when she thought of *The House is Black*. She believed that nothing was worth getting credit for too long, especially a naive movie like this. Moreover, not having any news from Ibrahim had given her a sense of suffocation. "If I was in Tehran I'd come to the studio. If you weren't there I'd call your house, if you didn't pick up I'd hang around your place looking at the windows for any sign that showed life was going on as usual and then I'd be relieved..."

One or two letters later, she was in Pesaro for the opening night. "In the hall before the first movie, everywhere I looked there was just talking, weird clothing, strange hairdos, eating, and eating, and more eating ... until I saw Bertolucci and started feeling more at ease..." She sent a few more letters during the festival before travelling to London. She mostly talked about movies she'd watched at the festival and how she felt nervous about appearing in front of the audience and critics after the screening of her movie. I read those letters, some of them a few times, and threw them back in the mailbox for Ibrahim to pick up.

In all her letters, she expressed her love for Ibrahim, but it was only after reading one particular letter that I stopped returning her letters to the mailbox. "Love like milk congested in the breasts and not sucked out is cutting my chest open. If I'm born again in a thousand years I'll still love you. If wind takes away my ashes, if I am turned into nothing, I'll still love you. My dear Shahi, dear Shahi, dear Shahi!"

I wasn't going to pass that for Ibrahim to read.

"From what you wrote earlier, I've realised that you haven't received some of my recent letters. I don't know why. Maybe someone else gets them and doesn't pass them to you? I think you should blame the postman though. Last time I told you that I didn't like him and you asked me why? This is why!" In the rest of the letter she talked about her visit to the National Gallery in London, and how, staring at the painting of Leonardo da Vinci in which everything was dissolved in a light blue, she'd undergone something like a religious experience.

I had to return the letters eventually. I knew I had no choice. But I still held onto them for another day or two before I threw four or five letters all together into the mailbox. Then I went home, and a couple of hours later, called the studio to let Ibrahim know that I had a back pain and could not come to work for a while.

*

I returned to the studio after a week. For the first two days, I didn't check the mailbox. I knew that if I found any of her letters in there, I wouldn't be able to resist the temptation. On the third day Ibrahim asked me whether he had any letters or not.

He had. I took it back home and read it before I'd changed my clothes. "I'm evolving in the way I love. I feel like nothing can threaten my love because it has achieved a depth and maturity so that it stands above all menace. It has turned to be like my blood, my breath, like the pupils of my eyes. I don't want you just for myself anymore. No, I want you to be, just to be. Like the sun that as long as it exists there's light and hope…"

I didn't read the rest of the letter. My mind started to wander; images flashed through my head one after another, taking me through years of this obscure one-sided love, all the torments, troubles, betrayals and deceptions, and finally the sad realisation that I wouldn't be able to put an end to it. No more I could disregard what I'd tried to ignore till then: she didn't see me as a "man" (not even as a naive young man as I'd thought before) and she never would. I'd merely appealed to her motherly instincts, perhaps with my nervous behaviour around women in general and her in particular. To her, I was just a shy kid. That was why she always made sure that I never missed out on office parties, raises, and bonus payments for the New Year. I wasn't in charge—she was! She was the one who could end this, who could put me out of my misery, but how could she end something she did not know existed? On the very first day of her return, I knew I would be in the studio, impatient to see her. Pathetic!

When my mind returned to the room where I was sitting behind my desk with my head over my arms, the paper, wet with tears, was crumpled in my fist. The second page of the letter had been ruined. I could just throw it away; they would probably blame the postman. Instead, I found a similar paper. It was slightly brighter, but I didn't care. On top of the page I wrote, "The ink of my fountain pen is finished. Now I have to write with a pen which is going to make my handwriting look awful." Then I put the new paper on the old wrinkled one and tried to copy her handwriting, following every curve, every dot, every loop and stroke meticulously, until my fingers ached. The day after I took the letter to Ibrahim's office.

"This was in the mailbox for you."

"I've *just* checked it, nothing was there."

"I don't know."

"Isn't today your day off?"

"I had something to take care of."

*

"How was your trip?" I asked Forugh on her first day back at the studio. I was having my lunch in the kitchen and she'd come in for a smoke. Her hair had grown longer, reaching her shoulder now, and she wore a white floral lace-embroidered shirt.

She opened the window over the sink. "You look tired," she said.

"Couldn't sleep last night."

"Why?"

"It's all good now."

"My trip was alright. A bit too long. I think I shouldn't have gone to Germany from London."

"How was the festival?"

"A bit disappointing," she said and tucked her hair behind her ear. It had turned into a competition, between the French directors and critics led by Godard on one side, and the Italians on the other. If Godard left the cinema in the middle of a film, half of the theatre followed him. She hated this kind of attitude towards art, the ridiculous master and devotee games. Maybe she was wrong, but she thought the human condition had left cinema as an art form and it was being reduced to a mere search for new forms and techniques.

"No good movies then?"

"I didn't mean that," she said. She'd watched a few good ones, both in the festival and in cinemas across Europe. She loved *Africa Addio* by Jacopetti. It was as if the images could expand and contract and grow soft and hard in harmony with their concepts. Kilometres of corpses, decaying corpses, women, men, children—and vultures. Mass execution and massacre. "At one point, I thought I was going to throw up. Watching death makes you humble—" she tapped her cigarette over the sink to ash "—I also enjoyed watching Godard's *Pierrot the Madman*. But the audience whistled and booed so much that I wanted to stand up and shout, oh shut up you sons of bitches!"

"And of course *Cul de Sac* by Polanski," I said and immediately realised the stupid mistake I'd made. She'd mentioned it in one of her letters to Ibrahim as the best movie she'd seen in so long. "Ibrahim was telling the guys how much you loved it the other day," I explained. I could only hope that she wouldn't bring it up later.

"I think Eastern European cinema is the best at the moment, especially Polish directors. This trip reminded me of how much I want to work, of how much time I've wasted these past two years."

She took a step towards the table, crushed her cigarette butt in the ashtray, and said, "Why don't you go home and take some rest? You look like you could use a nap. I'll tell Ibrahim that you had to go." Then she left.

I lit a cigarette, my hand trembling. I should go and never come back. I knew that I wouldn't.

\*

I need a break, I thought. I went to the kitchen and started cooking. As a young teenager, I had seen my father as a solemn and spiritual man who was too wise to waste his words. A man who mostly talked through his wife if he had something to say to his kids, other family members, or neighbours. But as I grew older, as I observed him more closely, I started seeing an ordinary introverted man and thinking about his life made me sad. He seemed to have led a passionless life. No career-related ambition, no ability to form a close bond with anyone, neither wife nor children, family nor friends. It seemed nothing could spark true passion in his heart, not even literature or gardening. Literature had been reduced to a career and gardening to a way to kill time.

Now I knew that in his own twisted fashion, he'd experienced passion at some point in his life, that he'd expended all his passion on his obsession with Forugh, and not much had been left to spare.

"I'm not sure if I want to hear your story anymore," I said, as I put a pot of fried rice on the table.

"It's not going to take much longer, my son," he said. "I promise."

We ate our lunch in silence—*patient, grave, confused.*

Father took a nap after lunch. Then he had a long shower. Finally, he sat on the balcony, placing his chair so his back was facing me. There is something you are reluctant to say and I'm not interested in hearing, I thought. Why don't we stop now, before it's too late?

# Chapter Eleven

Forugh read to me a poem named "Let Us Believe in the Beginning of the Cold Season." I'd read bits and pieces of it in her notebook as I stood over her bed that drunken autumn night.

*And this is me*
*a lonely woman*
*at the threshold of a cold season*
*coming to understand the soiled existence of the earth*
*and the sad innocent despair of the sky*
*and the impotence of these concrete hands.*

The poem was long and at times convoluted, and I couldn't stay focused. However, two particular stanzas attracted my attention, and got me thinking.

*And my wounds are all from love,*
*from love, love, love…*
*And how the trace of five branches of your fingers*
*—which were like five words of truth—*
*have marked her cheeks.*

*

A few weeks later when Forugh went to lunch at her mother's, Ibrahim asked me to pick her up so we could collect a reel of film from another studio. I drove in silence. Her expression was sombre. Another phase of depression? Something about her red eyes and the way she uttered her words—every word taking its time, sitting on her lips longer than it should before departing—gave me the impression that she was on some sort of a drug. I couldn't be sure though. My mind revolved around a question I'd been pondering for a while—the question that listening to her latest poem had evoked.

"Did he slap you?" I finally asked.

She snapped out of her reverie. "What?"

"Has he ever slapped you?"

"Once."

"What for?"

"I wish I could be just a housewife or something. Cook, clean, eat, sleep with my husband once a week, give birth and raise my kids," she said. "Being a housewife is the easiest way of life for a woman. Maybe I lack something. I am always looking for love and complete intimacy, to give myself to love in a way that you can give yourself only to death." Maybe that explained the challenging emotional life she had. Every time she tried to be just a simple woman, no ambitions, no complications, she started despising herself.

"Are you thinking of leaving him?"

"No."

The tremor in her voice made the uttered "no" sound unconvincing. Or maybe I wasn't convinced because I chose not to be. We didn't talk anymore, but her last word—compelling or not—triggered a rage in me, which was heavy with the years of suppression, longing, jealousy, and confusion, a rage that was becoming harder and harder to restrain. I was angry with myself, with her, with fate, with life…

"I'll be back soon," she said after I parked the Jeep.

I nodded. If I opened my mouth, the fury inside me, banging at my clenched teeth, would pour out. When she disappeared inside the studio, I got out of the car and kicked the driver's door before I took out the tiny knife given to me by Entezari years ago (which I'd attached to my keychain). I flicked it open and struck the car tire. The feeble blade snapped out of its pivot and hit my chest and then the ground. I hurled the handle at the sidewalk before taking her silver pendant out of my pocket and throwing it into the car. Enough is enough! I started striding away, not knowing where I was going. I hesitated, turned back and picked up the knife handle. I still needed my keys.

That evening I was about to call the studio to quit my job when the phone rang and I heard of the accident. Why was she behind the wheel? Why had I left her to drive when she obviously shouldn't have? Forugh had sent me on an errand, I lied. She'd asked me to buy some pain killers from a nearby pharmacy while she picked up the reel of film, and when I returned she'd driven away and left me behind.

I never found out what the real cause of the accident was. I'd changed the tires a few weeks back and they were too solid to be slashed by that dull rusted blade. Perhaps it happened like this: she was driving back towards the studio—fast; the way she loved to drive when she was down as if trying to leave her sorrow behind. She noticed her silver pendant under her feet, the one she'd been missing for so long. Without thinking, she stretched her hand down and reached for it. The pendant, the talisman for the evil eye, was in her hand as she raised her head and saw a bus turning in at the junction… That image of her reaching for the pendant has haunted me since and hasn't faded but grown more prominent by time.

I didn't cry when I heard the news of her death. Years of yearning for her had dried me of any tears. The curse was lifted. My suffering was at an end. At least I naively thought so.


The day after Forugh's burial, three days after accident, I returned to the studio to inform Ibrahim that I wanted to quit. I couldn't find him in his office. He was in the studio and would be back in his room soon, I was told. I went to the washroom and saw him standing in front of a mirror, his face covered in tears. He snapped out of it, bent over the sink, and splashed water on his face. I left without saying anything.

I returned to work the day after. I was watering the flowers in the office when Ibrahim asked if I could drive him to the graveyard.

During the trip, I asked, "What was the cause of the accident?"

"Speeding, I was told. She wanted to avoid hitting a school bus, the car skidded to the sidewalk, and hit a wall. She must've been thrown out when the car hit the curb, since I found her on the ground. Only a hundred meters from the studio. God! A few more seconds and she'd have been safe."

"Nothing was wrong with the car?"

"It's unlikely, you serviced it four weeks ago. I always told her not to speed and she never listened."

"What happened to the car?"

"What? Why?"

"I know it's not the right time, but I've lost a necklace that has a lot of sentimental value to me, and I had it on me that day before getting into the car."

"It was totalled. The police gave me a few items in a plastic bag and I signed for them, but no necklace was there, I'm sure. You could go to the car graveyard, if it means that much to you."

"That's alright," I said. I'd already searched the location of the accident.

Over the next few weeks I drove him to visit Forugh's grave a few more times. I always waited for him in the car and we seldom talked. During our last trip together, however, he asked, "Did you go to her funeral?"

"No."

"Me neither. What was the point of seeing her going under?"

On the way back, he spotted two of his acquaintances, a couple in their mid-forties and asked me to stop and give them a ride. In the car, the woman talked about their plans to move to a bigger house in a posh neighbourhood when Ibrahim barked at her out of nowhere, "Why are you alive? Huh? Why are you alive when she is dead?"

"I'm really sorry," he said a few seconds later to the stunned couple. No one said another word during the trip.

"I've found another job. I'd like to quit, if you don't mind," I said when we returned to the studio.

"Alright. Come by later in the week to pick up your last cheque," he said and walked in.

I sat on a bench in front of the studio, where I'd lounged around and smoked cigarettes for the last few years. I lit one last cigarette and imagined Ibrahim running out of the studio, picking her up, carrying her in his hands to a hospital just a block away, where she wasn't admitted because it was strictly for blue-collar workers. Even Ibrahim pleading "But she's dying" didn't change anything. Ibrahim, driving to the next hospital, turning and looking at Forugh's body in the backseat every few seconds, calling her name, trying to…

*Perhaps the truth was those two young hands,*
*those two young hands,*
*which were buried under the unceasing snow.*
*And next year, when spring*
*sleeps with the sky beyond the window*
*and her body spouts*
*green fountains of light branches,*
*she will blossom, dear yaar, the dearest yaar.*
*Let us believe in the beginning of the cold season.*

And then write poetry like "that". Like an oracle. Oracle of life. Death. Rebirth.

*

*My death will come one day, in a bright spring*
*in a winter, dull and distant*
*or in an autumn emptied of passion and joy.*

That was what I murmured when, after two months, I finally paid her grave a visit. Late at night, when nobody was around. I stayed there in silence. Staring at the tombstone that had no writing, no date.

*Perhaps at midnight my lovers,*
*place roses on my grave.*

I had no roses with me. That was the only time I saw her grave in person.
When I saw a picture of it almost a decade later, it had a proper stone with a
name and a date, and the poem "Gift" from *Another Birth* was carved on it.

*I'm speaking of ultimate night,*
*of ultimate darkness,*
*and I'm speaking of ultimate night.*
*If you came to my house,*
*oh you, the compassionate,*
*bring me a light,*
*and a window,*
*to look through*
*at the crowd of the blessed street.*

\*

I felt as if I'd swallowed a bit of darkness, as if a spot on my heart had irre-
versibly turned rancid and rotten. He sat there in silence—hands clasped
together in his lap, head bowed—as I hastily got ready and dashed out of
the apartment. It was almost dark outside, a curious sultry night. I strode
through the streets, counting my steps as I did when I felt anxious. Three
thousand four hundred and twenty steps later, I was still restless. The sweat
ran down my body, but I couldn't perspire away my anxiety.

I passed by a bar. I could've used a drink, but if I started, I wouldn't be
able to stop. I kept on walking, and the more I thought about his story the
more indignant I got. I felt as if I'd been cheated out of my peace, the fragile peace which, after Payam's tragedy, had taken a long time to acquire,
and a lot of discipline to maintain. What was I meant to do now? I didn't
want to think about it! I didn't want to think! Period!

I stopped at a dark corner of a park. There was no one in sight. I was as alone as the moon hanging majestically above the gum trees, like a portal of light tunnelling to another world, a better world, through the dark sky.

I opened my wallet and looked at the single stick of a cigarette that had been sitting there for almost two years now. I lit it and took a few drags greedily before I crushed it under my heel. I'd promised Ellie not to smoke. I had a sudden urge to see her, to hear her voice, but I didn't call her. What if I cried? What if I cursed him? I continued walking. I'd heard something dreadful. I knew it wouldn't leave me alone. Not now. Not soon. Not ever.

I could see some elements of my own personality in the story, which made it more confronting. I recalled falling in love for the first time as a teenager. My mother and I went on a five-day tour to Tabas, the city of bitter orange blossoms. There was a girl in our group, and the moment I saw her, I fell in love with her. During the trip I didn't dare to make a move. When we returned to Mashhad, her father picked her and her mother up from the travel agency and as he drove away I stood there angry with myself for being so hopeless.

I couldn't stop thinking about her. But I only knew her name and in the pre-social media era had no means to find her. Wherever I went, I kept looking for a blue scarf, the colour she'd worn during the trip. Blue was the colour of the day, so I experienced many short-lasting moments of hope that were shattered. Then one day, while cycling, I saw something I wasn't looking for: an old white Mercedes, the same kind as her father, and the bald man driving it *was* her father.

I started following the white Mercedes on my bike. Thanks to the congested traffic and favourable traffic lights, I was able to follow the car until it stopped in a driveway. I cycled there every day, and then up and down the alley in hope of… I didn't know in hope of what. Once, while passing the house, I raised my head and there she was. Behind the window with her honey-coloured eyes and a big smile. I didn't smile back, kept cycling, went home and never returned. Many years had passed, and I still wasn't sure why. Why I didn't wave at her. Why I didn't smile back. Why?

Fuck it! I'm going to have a drink!

*

I could discern his silhouette on the balcony. It's past midnight! Can't you
go to bed already? I didn't turn on the light. I wanted to hide in the dark,
change quietly, lie on the sofa, and then bury myself under the sheet. I sidled
past the small table when my toe hit the sofa leg. "Fuck!" I shouted. "This
shitty studio!" He'd turned his head and was staring at me, I realised. His
face shone pale under the moonlight; I hadn't offered him any food. "Go
to bed, it's too late," I said in a lower tone still bitter with pain.

"Do you mind if I sit here a bit longer?"

I said nothing, flopped onto the sofa, and rubbed my toe.

"My son," he called me, after I'd changed my clothes.

I walked to the sliding door and stood there in silence before I said, "If
you have something to say, just do it. I don't have the whole night."

"I knew if I told you this, I would alienate you. One day when you have
your own kids, you'll understand what that means for a parent. That's how
I'm paying for my sins. Not that I had a day in which I didn't. I'd have
spared you this, if it was just about me. But it's about collective conscious-
ness of a nation and you were the only one I could tell."

I went back in. I sat in front of the TV, changing the channels without
watching, letting the meaningless noises and colours drown my mind. It
only worked for a few minutes. I thought of his sickly face, turned off the
TV and said, "Do you want some tea?"

He nodded approvingly. While the water was boiling, I looked for the
pictures of Forugh's grave on the net. It was almost as he'd described. However,
it had another name he'd failed to mention: her father. *Daughter of Colonel
Mohammad Farrokhzad* it read. I felt a sense of pride behind those words,
carved on the chillingly white stone to re-emphasise the father-daugh-
ter relationship. Was it because almost the whole nation had mourned
her death? Or because even Farah, the Shah's wife, had sent her condolences to her father? Considering her relationship with her father, whose
approval she craved her entire life and never got, I found that ironic. I had
another thought, which I found unfair, as it seemed more like a farfetched

speculation, but I still couldn't hold it back from popping up in my head. Was her father, somewhere deep inside, also relieved? She died, young and at her peak like a rock star, sparing him the shame and leaving behind all the fame and glory.

I took a cup of tea and some dates to the balcony, where he was sitting, pale and weary.

"Do you want to know what happened to Maleki?" he asked timidly, almost apologetically.

I want to hear nothing, not even a word! I thought and went straight to bed.

Insomniac, left alone with my thoughts, I ruminated on how the next twenty-something hours of his stay would look like in silence. What could I do? Leave the apartment and only return when he'd left? I got out of bed, went to the balcony, turned the chair away from him so to face the city, sat, crossed my legs and locked my hands behind my head. It can't get worse than this, I thought.

This time I was right.

# Chapter Twelve

Maleki was released halfway into his prison term. His heart condition had deteriorated and SAVAK was concerned he would die in prison. They didn't intend to make a "martyr" out of him.

Two or three months after his release, Amir asked me to pay Maleki a visit. I'd been in the car with Amir when he picked Maleki up from the prison. That night we hadn't said anything beyond small talk. Now I didn't feel like going. I wanted to stay in the grocery shop—where I was working again—for another two hours then go straight home to bed. Amir insisted. He'd been visiting Maleki in and out of prison regularly and I couldn't understand why he required my company all of a sudden. He wouldn't take no for an answer.

"What's Maleki been doing since he got out?" I asked.

"Al-e-Ahmad used his connections to pull some strings and get him a job in the Department of Publication and Translation at Melli University. Then he met with an American human rights activist, infuriated the regime, and was fired by the president of the University."

"He really knows how to piss the authorities off, doesn't he?"

"It seems so."

It was late for visitors and I could tell that Maleki wasn't expecting to see us. Amir passed him the bag of apples and a box of chocolate cake he'd brought along.

"How is your writing going?" Amir asked. Maleki had written a portion of his political memoir while in prison and now was working on the rest.

"It's alright."

Amir walked to his table, "Do you mind?" and skimmed through the bundle of pages on the desk. "Do you want me to edit it for you?" he asked and passed the draft to me.

"Maybe in a month or two," Maleki answered, and I noticed that something in Amir's face changed.

While they talked, I flipped to the middle of his memoir and read a paragraph about Maleki's first arrest almost thirty years ago. The officers were searching his room, going through the library. One of the agents took *Das Capital* out, leafed through it, glanced at the picture of Marx at the back of the book, and put it back on the library shelf. Then he took a chemistry book, printed in red, and threw it on the pile of suspicious books! The story was comical, but it didn't make me laugh. Instead, my brain hung on to the word red. *Forgive her, whom across her coffin, the red current of moon flows, and the turbulent fragrances of night, disturbs her body's one-thousand-year-old sleep...* And I knew my mind would go through Forugh's poetry looking for the word red until it had scanned every single poem, every single verse—even though I wanted it to stop. And for her voice to leave me alone.

"Are you alright? You look tense," Amir said.

"I'm okay. I just need some fresh air."

I left for the yard and lit a cigarette. I wasn't the only man who desired her, I thought. Maleki had published one of her early poems in his magazine *Nabard-e Zedengi*, and had a signed first edition of *Another Birth* in his library. What did Maleki, one of the most restrained men I've ever seen, feel about Forugh? Not about Forugh as a poet, but as an attractive woman? He must've felt something that lurked beneath the surface and tingled his skin. Even if he was twice her age, even if he loved his wife, even if he was too dignified to acknowledge it... The thought didn't console me, but embittered me further.

How would life be if we couldn't hide our feelings? It would be chaos. No wonder we evolved with the means to mask our emotions and desires. Did Forugh never really fit in because she was unable, or unwilling, to properly conceal herself in a society of veiled bodies, veiled voices, veiled thoughts? It was one of my first attempts to understand Forugh after her death. A process—as self-revealing and painful as it was—without which any closure seemed unattainable.

I pressed the cigarette butt on the wall and tossed it into the garden. I didn't want to go back inside, and even though I never smoked back-to-back, I lit another one. *Life is perhaps lighting a cigarette, in the languorous interval of two love-makings...* Damn it! It didn't matter where I was and what I did. I stepped on the half-burned cigarette and rushed back in.

"Feeling better?" Maleki asked.

"Your nose is bleeding!" I responded. Maleki touched his nose and ran for the toilet, tilting his head back. He came back with a bloodstained cloth in his hand, pressing his nose every now and then to make sure the bleeding had stopped.

"How are you?" Amir asked Maleki.

"I'm alright."

"Does that happen often?" I asked.

"It started more than a decade ago and happens now and then."

"With no reason?"

"I don't know. The first time it happened, I was in a meeting with Prime Minister Mosaddegh," Maleki said. Mosaddegh had decided to hold a referendum for the dissolution of parliament and then have another election. A mistake, Maleki believed. Without parliament in charge, the conservatives had a perfect opportunity to orchestrate a coup. Maleki couldn't convince him to change his mind. "The path you've chosen is going straight to hell, but we'll follow you nonetheless," Maleki had told him finally. "Your nose is bleeding, Khalil," Mosaddegh had responded.

"That path was straight to hell alright," Amir said. "He should've taken your advice."

"Even if he did, it might not have changed anything," Maleki said. "The British and the Americans wanted him gone. The Shah didn't like him and neither did the Soviet Union, nor the Tudeh Party. He was a man for no season, after all."

"You should see a doctor about it," I said.

"I'm going abroad to study," Amir said out of nowhere. "I've got a scholarship. I'm leaving in a week."

"Really?" I exclaimed. "And so soon?"

"I've known it for a while. I just … I just…"

"That's great news," Maleki said. "Is it from the government?"

"No. From the Sorbonne University."

"That's better. More reliable."

I knew Maleki said that because three decades ago he'd received a government scholarship to do his Ph.D. in chemistry in Germany. His scholarship had been discontinued after the embassy had tried to hide the truth behind a student's death, and Maleki had refused to stay silent.

"Congratulations," I finally brought myself to say.

The doorbell buzzed. "Have some cake," Maleki said. The bell buzzed again. Maleki looked at the door over his shoulder and through the window, but didn't make a move. "Anyone want more tea?" he asked, and the bell buzzed for the third time.

I saw Maleki pass the yard through the window. There was a brief exchange before he opened the door fully and let someone in. The man who followed Maleki in stood at the entrance, took a handkerchief out, and cleared the sweat that dripped down his forehead. His deep-set eyes landed on me, and my gaze slid down his face to his saggy double chin—sad and large as if it were a home to many un-cried sorrows. I heard his thighs rubbing against each other as he waddled past us in the living room. He stopped in front of a room halfway down the hallway. "Here," Maleki said, standing at the room entrance, gesturing with his right hand and the man—who had to squeeze himself between Maleki and the wall—turned, and disappeared inside. Maleki walked to the middle of the living room, and hovered as if he wasn't sure what to do next.

"Is this everything?" we heard the man shouting.

"There are some more in the living room," Maleki said. They were moving house, so he'd decided to sell some of his books. They were too much

trouble for Sabihe with all the cleaning, and too heavy to drag along wherever they went.

"These are good books, but I can't pay you much," the man said.

"What are you doing? You know that my father always had a thing for
your library," Amir said with a nervous smile. Maleki looked at the buyer
and then at Amir, not knowing how to respond.

"If you didn't want to sell them, why'd you drag me all the way here?"

"I'm sorry," Maleki said.

"You have no concern for people's time, huh?" the man said, rubbing
the sweat off his forehead.

"Don't talk as if you've travelled from another town. I've been to your
shop, it's just two blocks down the road," Amir interfered.

"I'm not talking to you. Mind your own business."

"This *is* my business!"

"No. This is *my* business!" He was indignant. I could tell that for him
it wasn't about books or money anymore; he demanded respect. Something that he thought he never received as he deserved, just because of his
appearance.

"Okay. You can have them," Maleki said to the buyer.

"*No*. He can't."

Something in Amir's tone made the room fall silent. The man left, mumbling and cursing under his breath. I heard him banging the door shut.
Amir walked towards the washroom. Maleki left, his head bowed as if
looking for something lost amongst the colourful flowers of the carpet; he
returned with a bottle of *araq* and a cup. He flopped down onto the sofa
and poured himself a shot.

"We should get going," Amir said when he was back. "I'll ask my father
to send a check for the books. I'll take them when I come to say goodbye."

"Okay. I'll box them up for you."

*

I accompanied Amir to the airport the next week. To make it easier for his parents he'd said goodbye to them at home. On the way, he stared out of the cab window in silence.

"All those buildings will be here when you're back," I said.

"You never know," he whispered.

We didn't talk anymore until he checked in.

"Would you do me a favour and visit Maleki sometimes?" Amir asked.

"I'll check on him whenever I can, I promise." I hadn't told him that I was weighing the idea of leaving Tehran for another city.

"A couple of years ago, I was still a young teenager, it was after the coup of 1953, Maleki had just been released from prison, and we had a gathering in our house," Amir said, as if confessing. Maleki told them that they shouldn't let hopelessness get the best of them, that they should analyse the situation by taking a historical perspective and stay optimistic. Someone said that he preferred to take a "geographical" perspective and go somewhere he could live in peace. Maleki responded that even a mule could take a "geographical" perspective and go wherever the grass was greener. However, they needed to stay realistic, and organised, and keep the powers that be in check.

"I think you've made the right decision," I said. "Plus, you'll be back before you know it." I had no faith in my words. We hugged goodbye. I stood there watching him walk away. *People, group of fallen people, low-spirited and drained and stupefied was going from one exile to another under the ominous burden of their corpses…* No! I lit a cigarette, started muttering a pop song that was on the radio all the time, and walked off. If I give it some time, she'll eventually leave me, I thought. I hadn't realised that she lived through her words now. Insuppressible. Free.

*

Two weeks after Amir's departure, I bought some apples, like Amir would, to pay Maleki a visit. I caught him as he was about to leave his house for a nearby bar. "Let's walk together," he said.

On the way, going through the park, branches were swaying back and forth, leaves rustling, wind wailing—the start of a storm. I zipped my jumper and Maleki buttoned his raincoat and started walking with a hand on his brown bowler hat. "Strange weather for the summer," he said, and we picked up our pace to reach the bar before it poured.

"Are you alright? You've lost weight," he said.

"I'm okay."

"Did you colour your hair?"

"No. It's turned yellowish for no reason."

"No reason? You should see a doctor. Meanwhile, watch your diet and sleep. By the way, how's your study going?"

"It took longer than it should've, but I finished it last semester."

"Looking for a job now?"

"Yes. But not in Tehran. I'd like to experience living somewhere else."

"What kind of a job are you looking for?"

"Teaching."

"I always found teaching very rewarding. You know the most important lesson a teacher can teach his students?" he asked. "To help them understand the importance of asking questions." He believed that we were born with an inherent curiosity. As kids we ask questions, sometimes surprisingly good ones. Then we go to school and swap that for lots of answers.

"Do you miss teaching?"

"Of course. But what can I do? I'm not allowed to teach anymore. Are you still working at the studio?"

"I quit a while back."

"It was an unfortunate accident. Were you and Forugh close?"

"Not really."

"I wrote a small piece for her fortieth-day memorial, but nowadays whatever has my name on it doesn't pass censorship, regardless of its content."

*Wind is blowing in the alley, this is the beginning of ruin, that day when your hands were ruined, wind was blowing too…* "No," I whispered. *O imprisoned voice, will not glory of your despair tunnel towards light through this despicable night? O imprisoned voice, the last voice of voices…* "No," I flapped my hand in the air as if swatting words away.

"Are you alright?" Maleki asked a bit surprised.

"Sorry. I'm a bit agitated these days," I said. I didn't say that I'd become afraid of the dark and of being alone. Which was why I was here in the first place; walking with him to a bar, the last place I wanted to be. Why I couldn't stand a moment of silence, and spent my free time in crowded places where my thoughts were drowned in noise and clamour. Why—embarrassed to leave the light on at night—I took a small torch to bed, left it on under my blanket, and stared at that glistering ray of light until I fell asleep.


From that day onward, every Thursday, I waited for him in front of his house, and then we walked to the bar where we did shots, water for me and *araq* for him, and ate the apples I brought. During those nights, after some small talk, and occasional exchanges of ideas on literature or politics, he asked me whether I'd managed to find a job yet, to which I answered "No," and I asked him how his political memoir was going, to which he answered, "It's alright." In less than an hour, he was drunk and we continued doing shots and eating apples in silence. When the last apple was gone, I walked him home, where we shook hands and said goodbye. During my last five months in Tehran, that was my routine almost every Thursday night.

One night after finishing the apples, he continued ordering shots. I couldn't have any more water and went to the toilet. As soon as I sat back down, he started talking about the famous split in the Tudeh Party. He paused, lost track of his thoughts, and repeated himself. I signalled the bartender not to serve him anymore and asked for a glass of water, which he drank slowly before we left. On the way back, we sat on a bench in a park so that he could catch his breath.

"You know what they did?"

"Who?"

"They had this article published in a newspaper that condemned the terrorist act and—"

"What terrorist act?" I asked.

"The attempt on the Shah's life," he answered. They'd used his name and those of a few other reformists, those who were part of the split, to sign it. A win-win game, they assumed. If the reformists denied the article, they'd somehow approved the assassination. If they kept quiet, they could be labelled as monarchists. That was how dirty those bastards played! "I'm talking about the head of the party, of course, not those…" He fell silent and then narrowed his eyes as if trying to remember something "…*and I'm coming from a world of apathetic thoughts and…*"

He'd tried to recite Forugh's poetry, and his drunk mind had failed him. I did it for him. "*And I'm coming from a world of apathetic thoughts, words, and voices, and this world is like a den of snakes, and this world is filled with echoes of steps of those, who while kissing you, weave the rope of your execution in their minds.*"

I stopped, but he was still nodding his head approvingly. I lent him a hand to get on his feet and we walked back home.

*

The next week in the bar was all drinking and no talking; he didn't eat any apples either. There was a man sitting next to us at the bar who tried to initiate conversation with Maleki with no success. Occasionally he would turn to Maleki to say something nonetheless. The scar on his left cheek, raw as if caused by an object not sharp enough for a clear cut, and the suppressed rage in his eyes unnerved me. Regardless, I tried to distract him from Maleki, but he wasn't interested in the words I had to offer.

"You don't like talking or you don't like talking to me?" he said to Maleki finally.

"I think he is—"

"I asked *him*!"

"No problem talking…" he said and fell silent again. I was looking for something to say when he continued, "I just don't like…"

"What?"

152

"Rhetoric, it's just … and you know?"

"I know what?"

"He's just too drunk. Have an apple," I said.

He pushed back the brown paper and got on with his drink.

"Come on! Time to go home," I said.

Maleki stood up and took out some money to put on the counter. A piece of paper, folded in four, dropped out of his pocket. He left for the bathroom. I picked up the paper and unfolded it. It was a two-page letter.

*To my dear friend Amir Pishdad,*

*Hope this letter finds you well. I'm waiting for my eye surgery and for a while I can't read or write much. I took a friend's dog for a walk yesterday. It reminded me of that beautiful summer day we took your dog for a walk in Paris. Every time I remember that day it brings a smile to my face. Anyway, enough of chit-chat and back to the business.*

*Almost seven years ago, I wrote a letter to former Prime Minister, Mosaddegh who even after years of house arrest, was still considered the spiritual leader of the National Front and was respected by friends and foes alike. At the end of the letter, I said that despite being sixty I was still fully committed to working towards the goals of the National Movement, i.e., social justice and independence. Even a year ago when Mosaddegh passed, despite the sadness that overcame me thinking about a great man who was denied a grave and had to be buried in his own living room, I still felt motivated to work, write, and organise. But recently my body has been failing me. Moreover, the system moves from dictatorship to an arbitrary rule, which makes political activities even more challenging. My hope is in people like you, my friend…*

I skipped a few paragraphs. *…Regarding your open letter to the Tudeh Party: on the one hand, there are certain wrongdoings you've accused them of, which I personally think are not fair. On the other hand, they have done some harm that you have failed to mention…* I skipped to the last lines. *…However, there are moments in which the part of me that refuses to accept defeat, that pushes me to work despite everything, tells me that I may live long enough to see the fruits of what I have worked for…*

The bathroom door opened. I folded the letter back up and passed it to him. He mumbled something, put it in his pocket, and we left the bar.

*

I met Maleki at his house after his eye surgery. His left eye was covered and bandaged by a plastic dome. Sabihe brought us tea and dried dates, then left us to talk.

"Without her, I was lost years ago," Maleki whispered.

"There are times I feel empty," I said to my surprise.

"There are times we all do, I suppose," he said. His first time in prison, they'd decided to read and discuss *Capital*. His wife arranged for a German copy of the book to be smuggled into the prison, where one of the guards hid it in a corner of the prison yard. During their break, five or six of them formed a human shield while somebody dug it out and smuggled some pages inside. He would read it, translate it and share it with others. After every session, they shredded the pages, grabbed a handful and while walking in the yard let the pieces slide out of their fingers. They were in prison for being "communists" while the prison yard had been literally covered in Marx's words. "During my time there I felt angry, sad, helpless, but somehow never empty. It's not about where we are, but what we do, I guess."

I nodded. The sound of *azan* from a nearby mosque reminded me of those days when I carried unwavering truth in my heart. The *azan*, the pale yellow light that shaded the room, and Maleki, bedridden, defeated by his body and ideals, added to my sense of futility. It must've shown on my face.

"Let me tell you a joke," he said. "A doctor advises one of his patients with high cholesterol to walk five kilometres every day. A few months later his patient calls him to say, I'm at the border now, what should I do next?"

I couldn't recall the last time I laughed, not just with my mouth but also with my heart.

"I have no sense of humour myself, but I appreciate it in others," Maleki said.

"It helps us keep going," I said.

"I think we can relate to comedy because tragedy, which we're accustomed to, is nothing but comedy pushed too far," he said. He knew this ex-army officer, Baharmast, who worked as a lawyer in the military court. He'd defended a couple of political activists in an honest and uncompromising fashion. He also liked to mock the court and its made-up charges in not-so-subtle ways. Of course, he was made to pay for that. Later on, he was accused of sexually assaulting a woman—though it was known he didn't even like women. A comedy. Then, based on that ridiculous charge, he was sent to jail for three years, became a hardcore drug addict after his release, and died alone. A tragedy. "Argh! I have a throbbing pain in my left eye," he pressed his right palm on his good eye.

"Do you have any painkillers?"

"Yes, but I have to wait before I can take another one."

"I'll leave you to take some rest then."

"We'll chat soon," he said. "And everything will be fine, my son," he smiled.

*

Over the next couple of months Maleki went downhill. He needed another eye surgery and I could see it in his face that he was sick of being sick all the time. Two weeks before leaving Tehran forever, I waited for him outside his house as usual. He didn't show up. I left without ringing the bell so as not to face his wife. She came across as one of those people who could see right through you and her presence made me uncomfortable.

I didn't want to leave without saying goodbye and the week after I returned again for the last time. After lingering around the house for a while, I decided to check the bar. On the way there, taking the usual shortcut through the park, I saw him sitting on a bench, his head hanging over his chest, his body tilted to the right. He'd started early. I woke him up, grabbed his arm and brought him to his feet. I'd walked him home many times before, but this time he felt heavier. I could see he was struggling to keep his eyes open, but it wasn't sleep, of course. It was much heavier than that. It was death seeping into his body with every breath.

Sabihe opened the door. Without a word, she grabbed his left arm; his son ran and took his right arm out of my hand. The door was closed on me. When it was open I could see boxes of books piled on top of each other in the living room.

# Chapter Thirteen

I'd booked a train ticket for the evening. My luggage was packed and ready in my room. After lunch, I leaned against the plane tree in front of our house to smoke a cigarette one last time. As a teenager, it had provided me with shade for hours of reading books and waiting for Forugh to pass by. A silent witness to my malady and ache.

On the street, kids—still in their school uniforms—had marked two goals with their schoolbags and were playing football. Amongst them, I recognised Hosein, Forugh's adopted son. From the very beginning, he'd moved to Forugh's parents' house since she was busy all the time. I remembered when Hosein had come to the studio with Forugh. Ibrahim was working on his latest film, *The Sea*. In one of the scenes Forugh was slapped by the male leading role a few times, to get the best take. Forugh pointed at the screen and said, "Do you see how this man is slapping your mum?" Hosein looked at the screen and then at her in perplexity and said nothing. There was something in Hosein's silence, confusion, and uncertainty that I'd related to.

I smashed the remainder of my cigarette, shoved it with my forefinger into the wet soil, and walked towards the kids.

"Hey. Do you remember me?" Hosein nodded. "Do you want to go for an ice cream?"

"Can he come too?" he pointed at another kid. He was taller, a bit older, with a fluffy teenage moustache.

"Sure," I said. We started walking together.

"Are you happy living here?"

"Yes."

"Do you miss Forugh?" I said, not knowing why I would ask a child such a question.

"Yes."

"You don't talk much, do you?"

"Why?"

"Nothing," I said. "And what's your name?" I asked Hosein's friend.

"Aria."

I spoke to Aria so as not to make him feel left out. However, there was something peculiar about the way he talked. It took me a while to pin it down. He didn't use any Arabic words, which made him sound pompous, especially for his age.

"Why do you talk ... like that?"

"My father says that everyone should talk like this. We are Persian, not Arab."

"But many of those Arabic words are part of our language, more than some dated Persian ones."

"Are you a Muslim?"

"Yes."

"That's why you're so in love with Arabs," he said, turned, and walked away. I was annoyed with his immature reasoning, with his naive search for purity. Nevertheless, I wanted to run after him, hug his tense and confused body and tell him that everything would be alright.

"Is he your close friend?" I asked Hosein.

"He's a nice guy. It's just that the other kids make fun of him all the time."

We walked for a while in silence until we reached the shop, where I bought an ice cream sandwich for him.

"Who's taking care of you these days?" I asked on the way back.

"Grandma Turan."

"Are you in touch with your parents?"

"I call them every month. I also write letters."

"They don't ask you to go back?"

"They say that they want me to study and be successful in the future."

"Forugh was a good poet."

"Yes."

158

"You should learn a couple of languages."

"Why?"

"So you can translate Forugh's poems. Then many people, all over the world, will be able to read her poetry and she'd be remembered. I think she'd like that. I think all artists'd like that. I guess that's kind of the whole point."

"Okay." He licked his ice cream.

"By the way, what's your favourite food?"

"Hosein!" we heard someone shouting. Turan ran towards us and slapped him before she got on her knees and hugged him tight. "Where have you been? I got sick with worry!"

We'd been away less than an hour, but there were no kids on the street anymore. "I'm sorry. I should've let you know first," I said.

*

I moved to Mashhad. I hadn't secured a job yet, but I couldn't stand living in Tehran anymore. A family friend, who was about to retire, told me that he might be able to get me a job in his high school to teach literature. That "might" was enough for me to relocate. He did what he could, but I had to teach in Neyshabur for a year before I was offered a teaching position in Mashhad. A couple of months after moving to Neyshabur, I married your mother, the niece of the same family friend who had offered me help to get a job.

I hadn't heard from Amir after he moved to France, except for two letters during the first year, so I was surprised when he phoned me in Neyshabur.

"Maleki's passed," he said.

"I'm really sorry," I sighed.

"I talked to him two weeks ago. He said that despite being old he was still looking to the future. His voice worried me, but I chose to look at his words. I should've come back. Now he's gone."

"He had a serious heart condition. You couldn't do anything. No one could."

"Did you know that when I left, I didn't even say goodbye to him?"

"Yeah," I said. He didn't ask me how I knew. I didn't hear from Amir again for three decades.

*

After the demonstrations of June 1963, I refrained from politics altogether and turned into a keen observer, a fan at most. In Mashhad my metamorphosis was completed. I turned into my father. I stuck to my own business, teaching, and did my compulsory religious duties. I visited Entezari every time I travelled to Tehran to see my parents, which wasn't that often, since they were coming to Mashhad for pilgrimage quite regularly. Two years before the Revolution, my parents relocated to Mashhad, as they'd always wished to live next to the Imam Reza Holy Shrine. When I drove to Tehran to help my parents move to Mashhad, I met Entezari for the last time.

It was after hearing the radio anchor reading the historic message "This is Tehran, the real voice of Iran, voice of revolution..." that I called Entezari, to congratulate him. He was beside himself. "The Islamic *Republic* of Iran! Finally!" he said, before we hung up.

Plato, previously hidden in our minds and souls without us knowing, was everywhere now.

*

I didn't talk with Entezari that often afterwards. As a well-known revolutionary figure, he was occupied by numerous responsibilities during the first few years after the Revolution. He was chosen as a member of the Assembly of Experts, which was in charge of drafting the new constitution. That was when Entezari managed to introduce the doctrine of *velayat-e faqih*, the guardianship of the jurisconsult, into the constitution. Now the Supreme Leader, Ayatollah Khomeini, had not only spiritual but also temporal authority. Every week, I watched Entezari's live sermons during his time as the imam of Friday Prayer held at the University of Tehran. He was actively involved in building the utopia for which he'd spent years laying down the theoretical foundations.

160

There were rumours that Entezari was the favourite candidate to succeed Ayatollah Khomeini and to become the next Supreme Leader. However, it didn't take long before tension between him and the regime started, and escalated faster than anybody expected. I wasn't surprised, though. He was still the same person I remembered: frank, uncompromising, and outspoken. He and the regime reached a breaking point when he objected to the execution of members of the Mojahedin-e Khalq Organisation in prison, approved by the Supreme Leader. Entezari was labelled a counter-revolutionary, his house was stoned by a mob of "common folk" who were concerned about "true ideals of the Revolution", and he was put under house arrest.

More than a decade later, two weeks before Entezari's death, we spoke for the last time. One of our common friends, who had come to pay pilgrimage to Imam Reza, brought me a letter from him. He said that Entezari had had a stroke and his condition was deteriorating. Apparently, he'd also had a heart attack two years earlier. He didn't have much time left. Since then, every time I feel down I read that letter. It still gives me hope and brings me joy. I can recite it word by word.

*In the Name of Allah, the Most Merciful, the Most Compassionate.*

*My dear son,*

*I hope you are doing well. During the last two decades, I have been facing many unjust accusations. Those in power did whatever they could to soil my name, simply because I dared to think independently and for them it is the biggest sin one can commit. I always talked to you about the importance of unity. But in our days and time uniformity is mistaken for unity.*

*I was accused of having sympathy for the Mojahedin-e Khalq Organisation when the same group had assassinated my own nephew. I just believed that the members of the Mojahedin-e Khalq Organisation who were already tried and sentenced to prison should not be tried again for treason and executed because their organisation had joined forces with the Iraqi army. You cannot be punished for someone else's wrongdoings even if you are affiliated with them. It has such a simple logic and is in agreement with our Islamic teachings. However, they chose to ignore it.*

*The most preposterous accusation was me being against velayat-e faqih. Me! The same person who has spent his life laying the foundations of the doctrine. I still believe in velayat-e faqih. But I do not believe that faqih is above the law; his authority and responsibility is defined by it. The vote of people is the basis of the government, I believe, and even the position of the guardianship is nothing but a contract between the people and a faqih who can be disposed by people at any time.*

*During my life, before and after the Revolution, I tried to defend people's rights and worked for the independence and honour of this country. I criticised the regime because I could not witness the principles of the Revolution being undermined. I have lived according to Quran, the tradition of the Prophet, peace be upon him, and my conscience. God is aware of what is in our hearts, and he himself would judge us on resurrection day, the only judgment that really matters.*

*You may wonder, why I am writing this to you then? Because you are one of the few people who I would care how they remember me after my death. Because you have always been my son, even when you distanced yourself from me and decided to take another path. I was disappointed at first, only because I missed our time together and your enthusiasm for knowledge and justice that brought me joy. However, you need to know that I am proud of you for maintaining a decent life. For living a humble life and doing the best you could away from the sound and the fury of power.*

*May Mercy and Blessings of God be Upon You,*

*Your father,*

*Hossein-Ali Entezari*

I called him the next morning. He could barely talk. When I wished him a prompt recovery he said, "This time, there's no recovery, my son."

"You'll recover soon, inshallah."

"First my heart and now my brain. These are vital for any system to be functioning properly."

I understood what he meant. "You're absolutely right," I said.

"I might be right. But I'm not *absolutely* right," he replied. I could picture him smiling at the other end of the line. I knew the conversation was being

162

taped, but there was a question that I wanted to ask him for years and this could be my last chance.

"Why did you object to the executions? Wouldn't it have been better for the people and the future of the country if you stayed in power?"

"There's no future if you can't sleep at night," he said. At this point of the conversation, I could hear him breathing heavily. "I never thought that one could lose by winning—" There was a long pause, a struggle to get oxygen in "—and win by losing."

\*

"This is everything," he said. "Everything which is worth saying."

I leaned back in my seat and took a deep breath. "What happened to Hasan? Are you two still in touch?" I asked.

"Let's talk about that another time," my father said. "It's way past midnight."

"You wanted me to hear your story and I'm listening now. Why don't you finish it?" I pushed despite (or maybe because of) his haggard face.

"Okay. Let's get it done with," he whispered, his eyes fixed on the floor, as if dreading the words that would follow.

\*

Hasan was among those members of Mojahedin-e Khalq who were tried again and executed when in prison in the summer of 1988. He was always anti-Shah, but he might never have become actively involved in politics if it wasn't for me. I introduced Hasan to Ayatollah Entezari whose political ideas gave him a direction and a sense of purpose.

There was more to Entezari's letter than the part I recited. It started talking about Hasan. He thought that I'd stopped contacting him because I blamed him for Hasan's death. Entezari had tried to postpone the executions to after the holy month of Muharram, hoping he could use the time to lobby. He did what he could, not just for the sake of Hasan but for justice, and failed.

I hadn't stopped calling him because I blamed him for Hasan's execution;

I knew his phone was tapped and I was afraid to have my name on a black-list. I still inquired about his wellbeing through our mutual friends and sent my regards. Maybe he didn't receive my messages, or assumed that I was just being polite. When I called him that one last time, I didn't dare to mention Hasan's name. I asked that question about why he didn't keep quiet about the executions partly to show him that I understood: that I knew he'd done more than most people would have.

After I relocated to Mashhad, I met Hasan every year for one week when he came to pay pilgrimage to Imam Reza and stayed with us. It was during his last visit before the Islamic Revolution when I learnt that he'd joined the radical anti-Shah organisation of Mojahedin-e Khalq. He did his routine of pilgrimage for another three years after the Revolution. However, when the president Banisadr was impeached by the parliament in 1981, the Mojahe-din-e Khalq Organisation declared war on the government of the Islamic Republic of Iran. Hassan was arrested shortly after. I was so worried he might be executed that when I received a phone call from his brother and learnt about his sentence, I was relieved. He wasn't directly involved in armed activities and assassinations and therefore was sentenced to eight years in prison. "He got lucky this time," his brother told me.

That luck didn't last for long.

When Mojahedin-e Khalq joined forces with the Iraqi army during the war, Hasan had two years before his release. He—like other political prisoners who were kept isolated from the outside world—hadn't heard of the act of treason committed by the Organisation. When he was taken to be re-tried, which was nothing but three questions to test his loyalty to the Organi-sation, he had no idea that answers to those questions would seal his fate.

I heard the news of his execution from his brother. That night, I lay in bed, sleepless, thinking about Hasan in prison, having his last meal, using his spoon to engrave circles on the wall of his cell. I got out of bed and walked to the front yard. I sat on the stairs and lit a cigarette, my first in seven years. I looked at the full moon, elegant and indifferent, and took a drag. "Vanity, vanity, it's all vanity," I sobbed.

# Chapter Fourteen

He stood up and walked to the washroom. He wasn't going to let me see his tears. The apartment smelled of him, of slow decay and pain. I wished I could bring myself to hug the old man and console him. I wished I could kiss his wrinkled face and tell him that all was good now, and he would have peace, and not just the one promised by his inevitable death.

I left the apartment, walked to a nearby gas station, and bought a pack of cigarettes. I lit one sitting on the ground, leaning against the glass window, hugging my knees, observing the slow nightlife that unravelled in front of my eyes, like a sad show of loneliness, insomnia, and unsatisfied cravings. A toothless and shirtless vagrant talked to an imaginary companion moving his hands franticly as if trying to convince the invisible man that he existed; a young girl wearing only a long white T-shirt that reached to her knees walked barefoot to the store, returned with two packs of gummies, and her red puffy gaze met mine before she got into a white van; a middle-aged man with horrified eyes, as if they had frozen right after recording a scene of terror, asked for a light.

I smoked another cigarette, and then one more. It seemed that now that I'd broken my promise it didn't matter how many I had. The first drag of the fifth one made me feel sick in the stomach, but I kept going. And when the nausea finally overcame me, I gagged and ran for a tree at the side of the road. The thin acidic fluid didn't expel any of my gloom. Perhaps the sorrow, the one I'd tried to escape my entire life, had finally became one with my heart.

When I returned home, I couldn't find him in the unit. Having remembered what happened a few days back, I dashed for the door without calling his name; then I noticed the light coming from under the bathroom door.

I found him lying in the bath, his eyes closed.

"Hello?"

It was as if he jolted awake out of a dream. "Can you help me? I sat down and I couldn't stand up again."

I knew it wasn't the whole truth. He covered his genitals with his left hand and offered me the right one. The water was cold. I passed him a towel before I brought the hair dryer over and blew some hot air on his body. I asked the question that I knew the answer to.

"What's going on?"

He hesitated for a moment. "You know what's going on, Saeed." He sat at the table.

"Are you…"

"Yes. I am."

"How long have you known?"

"Almost a year."

"Is there anything that can be done?"

"I'm taking some medicine, but it only slows it down."

"Do you want to consult a doctor, now that you're here?"

"No."

"There's no harm in seeking a second opinion."

"I know that when I'm dead, I'll be no different from this piece of wood," he said, tapping on the table.

"But you don't miss a single prayer!"

"I can only pray that I'm wrong," he smiled. His eyes glimmered with wisdom for a second before the darkness took over again. "A life without God is like a story with no closure. It's not for everyone," he murmured. A long silence. "During your youth, there are elements of the fear of death in the way you cling to your religious beliefs. Even though when you're young you don't think about death—not directly at least. When you're middle-aged, you wish for your youth, you secretly wish you would never die. When you're old you just want to be able to face it with serenity and dignity."

"Anything I can do?"

"I wish you could hold my hands when I'm walking to the dark side. But this is life. What can we do?"

"I can always come back."

"You can't take the risk."

"Nobody really cares about a damn novel."

"Maybe they do, maybe they don't, you never know. Sometimes nothing can make you discipline yourself like not knowing. I want you to do something for me though. The story I told you, I want you to write it down." He looked into my eyes.

I wasn't sure that I'd heard him right, and it took me a few seconds before I said, "I really don't know if I want to deal with—"

"I know that I'm asking for too much. But if you ever bring yourself to write it down, wait until I'm gone before publishing it."

"Okay," I whispered.

"I discovered her and God almost at the same time. She left me years ago. Now I'm losing my memory and with that God is abandoning me too. Do you remember I told you about the day when I followed her on the street? I told you she turned and I hid behind a tree. When you write that scene, I want her to see me hiding, to recognise me. I want her to smile before she turns and walks away," he said and his eyes shimmered with a passing excitement.

"Okay," I nodded, without being sure what I was exactly agreeing to.

*

I stared at the ceiling, sleepless. His breathing had turned to a faint snore while I tried to find a comfortable position. I removed the sheet and sat on the edge of the sofa. I could distinguish his silhouette, on his back on the bed near the balcony door. His torso was lit by moonlight, by billions of photons travelling millions of kilometres through space from the sun to the moon, only to be reflected again towards Earth. His legs were in the dark, representing those particles that had failed to finish their journey, foiled by the wall only a few metres away.

I tiptoed to my table, sat, plugged in my headset, and turned on my laptop. I typed, *The House is Black*. The movie popped up on YouTube. It was only twenty-two minutes.

Why a movie about leprosy, though? About outcasts? Had she felt like one herself? It couldn't be the only reason why she made that movie, but perhaps it was why she made it well. She understood the lepers and their world and in return they'd trusted her and let her be their voice.

"There's no shortage of ugliness in the world. If humans closed their eyes to them, there would be more… A dreadful image, a vision of pain will appear on this screen that no compassionate humans should close their eyes to. Finding a remedy for this unsightly condition and relieving the pain of its victims is the motive behind making this film and the wish of the producers," said the voiceover.

I sat there watching the movie, zoning in and out. In my reverie I saw him: staying behind the filming crew, leaning against a wall, lighting a cigarette, smoking away his unrequited love, watching Forugh as she talked to the cameraman, engaged with the lepers, planned the next scene…

"*Praise the Lord with the harp; make music to him on the ten-stringed lyre. I praise you because I am fearfully and wonderfully made*," her voice read over the images of day-to-day life in the asylum. In one of the final scenes of the movie, filmed in a classroom at the leprosarium, the teacher, wearing a white shirt buttoned under his Adam's apple, asked a student, "Why should one thank God for having a father and mother?"

"I don't know. I have neither," answered the student.

The teacher looked at Hosein and said, "Name some beautiful things."

"The moon, sun, flower, and playing," he answered.

"Name a few ugly things," the teacher asked another student.

"Hand, foot, and head," he answered, and the other students giggled. The teacher asked a student to write a sentence with the word "house" in it on the blackboard. The scene cut to community members seeing off the camera until a door closed down on them. Then a cut back to the classroom as the student wrote, *The house is black*.

I woke at 11:50am. I'd watched *The House is Black* twice, and then listened to Forugh reciting some of her own poetry. I went to bed again at 4:10 am, but the last time I checked my phone, frustrated with my insomnia, it showed 5:25 am.

My father was on the balcony drinking tea. "I thought we had a lunch appointment today," he said.

I texted Ellie and let her know that we might be fifteen minutes late.

We met Ellie at Ayla's café. Ellie wore her retro blue jeans and her favourite T-shirt of Pink Floyd's flying pigs, taking a break from being an environmental lawyer. He couldn't communicate with her beyond basics and I had to work as a translator between the two of them.

"Saeed didn't tell me that you're Chinese," he said at some point. Ellie's parents had migrated from Taiwan when she was two. I guessed that she would have recognised the word "Chinese" so I took the liberty to translate it as "He thinks that Chinese girls are beautiful."

"You yourself are good-looking too. Now I know from whom Saeed has got his good looks."

He asked Ellie about her job and a few questions about her family. She seemed happy that he'd taken an interest in her personal life. "I think your son is a great guy. I do love him," Ellie said with a smile.

"Very good. But I personally think that love is overrated."

It took me a second or two to come up with, "I think every relationship should be based on love."

Ellie's eyes shone and she smiled at him before she tilted her head towards me to kiss me. I pretended I hadn't noticed that, pushed my chair back and stood up. "Time for shopping now," I said and smiled at Ellie.

He bought some clothes for my mother and some packs of tea for his friends who he caught up with in a nearby park for a chat each day before they went to the mosque.

"We did some good shopping today," Ellie said.

"Thanks to you," I said.

"I've got you something." She offered him a paper bag. Inside was a green woollen scarf she'd bought from Puppy Pound, her favourite vintage shop. "To keep you warm in winter."

His face showed that he'd appreciated the gesture. "Thank you," he said.

She hugged him goodbye, which made him uncomfortable, but less than I thought it would.

"Take good care," she said.

"You too. Take care of yourself and Saeed. I'm happy he has you."

He said the last sentence in English. Ellie's face brightened. She hugged him again. We watched her walking off for a second and then turned away.

*

"Sorry for some of the stuff I said. I didn't mean to embarrass you."

"It's okay," I said. We were sitting on a bench in a park. He'd asked for green scenery and fresh air before being confined in a cage for thirteen hours.

"I'm too old and I just say whatever comes to my mind."

"Forget it."

"You did the right thing. Changing some of my words, I mean. She looks like a nice girl."

"I just don't know what you meant by love being overrated. You don't believe that people can love each other?"

"Yes, they can. But for a relationship to work you need more than love. Love withers over time; that's its nature. And there's one more thing that I've understood about love. The afterlife to life is like love is to sex."

"What do you mean?"

"Doesn't matter. Do you remember the first computer I bought for you?"

"Yeah. A Pentium III, the latest model at the time."

"You taught me how to use the computer and the internet and made me

171

an email account. Forugh was the first name I searched for. I found a biography of her by an American professor. I asked Amir to post it to me. Two years before, he'd surprised me with a visit. It was his first time back home after the Revolution. He was running some workshops on the philosophy of non-violence at the University of Tehran."

"Did you read the book?"

"With a dictionary at my side it took me a year to finish it. Did you know Forugh was learning painting from Katuzian for a while during her teenage years?"

"*The* Katuzian?"

"Yeah. During a session, after she finished a painting, Katuzian tried to make some corrections. She objected that he wanted to force her to paint like him, left, and never returned. A fourteen-year-old! That was why she never got intimidated by big names or spellbound by any ideology. Why at the end she was like no one else but Forugh Farrokhzad."

"You should've told me about Amir's visit."

"You were at the University of Tehran at the time."

"Exactly! I could've gone to his lectures."

"I preferred that you stayed away from any activities that could've been labelled as political. Amir passed me a draft of the biography he was writing on Khalil Maleki, but we never got a chance to really talk about it. Shortly after, he was arrested and interrogated by the Ministry of Intelligence, being accused of participating in a colour revolution to overthrow the Islamic Republic. He was released three months later, mostly because of national and international pressures, and left Iran in a hurry."

"I vaguely remember my friends talking about his trial. Did you like the book?"

"I wrote to him about what I thought of it. He said he'd only publish it if he thought he'd done Maleki justice. I'm not sure if he ever did."

"I could check it online."

"I think it's time we left."

We sat at the only free table at the airport café, near the entrance. He took an aspirin with his tea.

"Is there anything you'd like to ask me before I leave?"

"If there is, we can always talk over the phone."

"I knew things wouldn't be the same."

"I just need some time," I said. I needed much more than that: to open my eyes at some point and realise that everything had been a bad dream. And by everything I didn't mean only his story, but the last fifteen years of my life, or maybe even before that—long before. Time could heal every despair, I'd heard. What about the despair rooted in my body, in my genes which fed and grew on everything that preceded it: history, culture, and all the surrounding material factors. For me, the only possible cure was the impossible metamorphosis of body and soul.

"There's one last thing." He passed me a folded paper. It was brown and covered in yellow spots. I unfolded the battered, saw-edged paper slowly. I could barely read anything save for a few words. It was the handwritten copy of "Sin".

"Wow!" I said involuntarily.

I looked at his hand reaching into his pants pocket again, and thought, what's next? He put the tiny handle of a switchblade knife on the table. A keychain was hanging from it. The blade was missing.

"I don't even know why I'm giving you these. I can't stand the thought that after my death when your mother's sorting my stuff out, even if she notices them, she'll dump them. Maybe they can inspire you one way or another if you ever choose to write the story."

I sat there staring at the handle of the knife and I wanted to ask… And I remembered "Thou shalt not ask!" I refolded the paper and placed it in my shirt pocket. I put the handle in my pants pocket.

He took out a pill and swallowed it on the first sip of the second cup. "Can you get me some water please?"

I came back with a bottle and poured him a cup. With every sip the wrinkles between his eyebrows deepened, and the corners of his eyes narrowed as if he was contemplating something. Though I wondered what, I didn't ask. I'd already had enough.

"You know what made her different from her contemporaries," he said as if talking to himself. "She was a believer. She left the certainty of her comfortable domestic life and walked right into the darkness, when the one thing she was certain of was what she *didn't* want to be for the rest of her life: a housewife. She longed to turn herself into someone or something of which she had no clear idea. Only a true believer takes such a leap of faith." He put his cup down and we got on our feet. "I'm sorry for the pain my story has caused you."

I had this image from my childhood. He was sitting next to the heater in the living room, my head rested on his lap. He was sipping tea and reading poetry, stroking my hair. "We learn and grow through pain," I said. "There seems to be no other way. Let's go."

We were in the queue when I realised that I didn't have my mobile. I rushed towards the café and found it sitting on the table next to the pot. I was about to leave when I noticed an ink-stained, crumpled tissue paper on the floor. I picked it up and spread it open on the table. It was written on with a fountain pen. The words weren't clear, but I still managed to read it. It was in Farsi.

*A cup of tea,*
*fragrance of cinnamon,*
*apple-flavoured steam defying gravity,*
*playful patterns by the warm sun on the table,*
*a leap inside me to feel blessed,*
*a happy fall!*

I folded the tissue and put in my pocket, next to the handwritten copy of "Sin".

I watched him going through customs. He looked smaller than ever, his coat hung from his gaunt shoulders, embracing him like a child.

*There is an alley*
*where the boys who were in love with me, still*
*with the same tangled hair and slim necks and thin legs,*
*are thinking of the innocent smiles of a girl*
*who was taken away with the wind one night.*

He trudged a few meters forward, stopped, turned and waved goodbye. I waved back. "Baba …" I wanted to shout, "It was not worth it."

He nodded, as if he'd heard the thought. The shadow of a smile appeared on his face. "You've taken a leap of faith, my son," he said. His eyes shimmered like the prayer beads in his hand.

I knew I would not see him again.

# Acknowledgments

The idea to write a novel about the contemporary Iranian poet, Forugh Farrokhzad, was formed during a talk with my uncle, Jafar Sarve. However, *Only Sound Remains* might never have been written if it were not for the PhD position at the University of Adelaide and the RTPS scholarship I was awarded. For that, I would like to thank Brian Castro and those in the Department of English and Creative Writing who gave me the opportunity to undertake a Ph.D. in Creative Writing and to be part of the J. M. Coetzee Centre for Creative Practice, for four wonderful years. Many thanks are due to my supervisors, Jennifer Rutherford, Rachel Hennessy, and Jill Jones and to my friends, Gemma Parker, and Benjamin Nicholls, who supported me during my study and while rewriting the novel.

Many great books and writers helped and inspired me. Two amazing biographies guided me as I tried to understand the life, times, and poetry of Forugh Farrokhzad: *A Lonely Woman: Forugh Farrokhzad and Her poetry*, by Michael Hillmann; *Forugh Farrokhzad: A Literary Biography with Unpublished Letters*, by Farzaneh Milani. The latter is the source for the letters I have used, for which I am grateful. I became familiar with Khalil Maleki and the important role he played in politics of his time through a number of brilliant books by Homa Katouzian: *Khalil Maleki: The Human Face of Iranian Socialism*; *Political Memoire of Khalil Maleki; Letters of Khalil Maleki*; and *A Eulogy for Khalil Maleki*. The character of Amir came to me after reading the inspiring *Time Will Say Nothing*, by Ramin Jahanbegloo. The verses from the Quran are taken from *The Message of the Qur'an*, an English translation and interpretation of the Quran by Muhammad Asad. For the verses from the Bible, I have used the *New International Version*. The translation of Farrokhzad's poetry is mine and so are the shortcomings.

Special thanks to my publisher and editor Ed Wright whose insightful feedback has truly made a difference in the quality of this book. Finally, my love and gratitude to Elizabeth Chang without whose encouragement I would have never started this venture.

www.ingramcontent.com/pod-product-compliance
Lightning Source LLC
Chambersburg PA
CBHW032119020726
47494CB00007BA/2151